Also Available From Jacy Morris

One Night Stand in Ike

By Jacy Morris

Table of Contents

Prologue: An Easy Journey

Yokel stood dazed in the middle of Shithole, plucking at his crusty, homemade T-shirt. The town felt different, as if the heart of the settlement had been scooped out with a spoon when the comedian made his exit. The citizens of Shithole walked with their heads down, their eyes on the tips of their dusty boots.

Overhead, the sun shone orange through the burnt world-haze that drifted across town. Murdertron was gone. Beatums was gone. The sheriff had left that morning.

Among the spindly trees and the reek of the shit pile out back, Yokel spun in place. Shithole was dying; the signs were everywhere.

In the gray ramen of his brain, filled with Swiss cheese holes from chugging radiator fluid for a good portion of his life, he envisioned the town rotting slowly, the metal signs of the walls rusting and corroding into nothing, the wooden timbers eaten away. As he spun, the entire town crumbled into disrepair. The people disappeared, dragging their meager possessions behind them until Yokel stood alone, in a town once called Shithole. The sun arced overhead, over and over again, and the world alternated between day and night, the years passing by as the tumbledown shacks returned to the earth. Who was to say how long into the future Yokel went, but there came a time when the sun slowed and the cycle of night and day returned to normal, and Yokel stood in the middle of a small forest of tall trees, their trunks as thick as his body swaying in the wind.

"No sign. Nothing." *It's like I never existed.* But Yokel had existed in this world, had experienced its horrors and its gifts, its pleasures and its sadistic tendencies. That his life should vanish without a trace was the biggest travesty of the entire world in his humble opinion.

He blinked, and the town reappeared, the citizens dragging heels through the dust of Shithole once more.

Already carrying everything he owned on his back, Yokel shrugged and left Shithole. It was going nowhere, quite the opposite of the life Yokel envisioned for himself.

He stepped through the town's gate, shutting it behind him. With nothing more than the clothes on his body and a jagged length of twisted, rusty metal to his name, Yokel took his first steps toward the wastes.

That's where he went, him and Beatums.

Yokel had seen greatness, back when he had gone by the name Tony, back when cities had risen into the sky and thousands of humans crawled among their great edifices like ants. He had seen greatness in the dark, amid the whirring of film through projector innards, 35mm greatness, actors playing roles, artists crafting gore-filled spectacles to fuel nightmares. Little did they know how accurate those spectacles had been.

When the world broke, Yokel had seen how correct those latex and corn syrup tableaus were. Amid a gaggle of lost wanderers, Yokel had watched, one by one, as the people he knew, the people he'd fled Denver with, were devoured, burned, hunted, melted, disemboweled, and sometimes vaporized. Soon, it was just him, walking and wandering, tapping the radiators of vehicles left to rust and rot amid the harsh sun. During these meanderings, he had wished for death, but though the world was filled with monsters and the earth itself wanted to kill everyone and everything, nothing ever happened to Yokel.

Then, with his brain melted and devolved, he had stumbled upon Shithole. How long ago? It was hard to say, and as he thought, a blinding, searing pain made him squeeze his eyes shut, as if he had poured sugar on a deep, tooth cavity. He'd tried to access one of the memories in his brain that no longer existed, one of the places where the chemicals in the radiator fluid had left a bank of dark cells, dead and beyond resurrection.

But he was sure years had gone by, and though he kept himself purposefully distant, he had cultivated working relationships with the townsfolk. Sure, some of those relationships consisted of getting rapped on the knuckles when his sticky hands touched some bit of merchandise on Murdertron's table. Some of those relationships consisted of dodging the rocks the kids threw his way. Some of his relationships consisted of women holding their noses as they walked past his ripe body. Despite how pathetic all those interactions were, they were still interactions, and he wanted them to continue, but not here.

Yokel stopped at the edge of the green grass surrounding Shithole. He squatted down and held out his hand to the blades. They writhed and twined about his fingers. "I'll miss you, buddy."

He let the grass tickle the pads of his fingers as he surveyed the world spread out before him. *East? Yeah... maybe.* Yokel looked up at the sky, clocking the sun and trying to figure out what it meant and how some people could use it to navigate. He shrugged, pet the grass one more time, and stepped into the wastes.

****

Every unlucky traveler who had appeared out of the wastes spoke of deadly creatures, an environment capable of killing an unwitting traveler in the blink of an eye or three. Other than the sunshine, which threatened to crisp up Yokel's fair skin, he didn't see what all of the fuss was about.

As far as he was concerned, the wastes were a walk in the park. He spent half of the first day, traveling through a beautiful green field dotted with Skittle-colored flowers, their fragrant bouquets tickling his nose. Among the flowers and grasses, chipmunks skittered about, bouncing along without a care in the world. He admired their simplicity, and when the field gave way to an environment more like what he envisioned for the wastes, he was sorry to leave the playful creatures behind.

His first step into the waste proper was met with nothing more than a cooling breeze and the kiss of sunshine through the clouds above.

As he traveled, Yokel plotted ways to ingratiate himself to the comedian, and if the comedian wouldn't have him, then maybe Beatums would agree to his company. Either way, he wanted to be near their greatness. Sometimes, you couldn't be the fire, but you could get warm standing next to it. By himself, he was incapable of leaving his mark on the world, but among the company of greatness, he might be able to leave a footnote somewhere, even if it meant risking his life.

Although, if this is all the world has to offer, he didn't figure his life was at much risk at all. The waste was dry, certainly, but in an abandoned apartment complex out in the middle of nowhere, Yokel found a stash of water bottles full of the good stuff. He plucked a backpack from a hall closet, dumped them in, and then he was good to go.

Time passed on and on, and though the sun never lessened, its strength never ebbing, he made good time. The miles passed by, and he had never breathed so easy. Even though he thought he would, he didn't miss the ever-present stench of human manure. Heck, out here among the warm dry breeze and the sunshine, he didn't even miss any of the people. Letting his feet take him where they would, Yokel strode on, fine-tuning his hype-man spiel, adding words and emphases where he could.

The man, skinny and somewhat sunburned by this point, was practicing exotic, showman-like hand gestures

9

when he stumbled onto a field full of green plants. All around, vegetables grew so fast he could almost hear their skins stretching as they expanded. He plucked a few and placed them in his backpack. Thinking maybe he had found a new home, he bent down to pet the grass, but it sat there, still and immobile. He shrugged and moved on, never noticing the pair of eyes watching him as he hiked out of the valley.

Then he passed a set of hills just as pretty as anything he'd ever seen, rounded and all sorts of different colors, like the inside of one of those giant novelty jawbreakers they used to sell. At first, he thought his eyes were playing tricks on him, but as he neared them, they stayed the same. He drank an entire bottle of water and sat in the shimmering desert heat staring at those hills. When the bottle was empty and the last drop of water had dripped onto his tongue, he placed the empty bottle in his backpack and moved on.

Next, he came to a town called Itch, a funny name for a town if he'd ever heard one, although he had just come from a town named Shithole. *What if the two towns joined together? Then it'd be Shithole Itch.* Chuckling to himself, he strolled through the sleepy, desert town, marveling at how the buildings still stood. It looked like an old western town, and he imagined somewhere in the small town would be a saloon where a crusty old bartender served firewater and cowboys playing poker sized up anyone who strolled through the batwing doors. But no, this was Itch, not Ike, so he moved on, wandering through the town and ignoring the calls of the raiders within.

The raiders, deterred by the obvious insanity of the wanderer and the lack of meat on his bones, didn't even bother with him. The day was too hot.

On Yokel strode, striding across old highways that had turned into dry river beds for the random rain the wastes received once a year. His boots felt good on his feet,

10

and in no time at all, he came to his destination. He arrived so quickly and with so little trouble Yokel was forced to stop in front of the town and turn around.

"Huh," he said to himself. "I thought that would be tougher. Shrugging his shoulders, Yokel knocked on the doors of Ike, a toothy smile on his face. As he waited, an idea crossed his mind. *A cinematist! I can be a cinematist! T.C. can't say no to that.*

The smile stayed glued to his face as he introduced himself to the people of Ike.

Chapter 1: The Road to Ike

The comedian hated the wastes. In all his travels, he had never experienced such an inhospitable chunk of land. After dodging evercracks and shriekers and your run-of-the-mill cannibal raiders, he was looking forward to reaching their destination. The only trouble was he didn't know how much longer they had to go.

To his right, Ajax walked—always on his right. She thought he didn't know the reason why, but he knew exactly why she did this. It was because, if for some random reason, he decided to attack her while walking, she could defend herself with her mace. If she walked on the left, it would be that much harder to defend herself.

His traveling companion was not an idiot, and he knew she would be a tough fight if he ever decided he didn't want her tagging along. But, according to her theory, those who traveled together held back the wastes, kept the decay of the world at bay. He didn't buy her theory, but if it made her feel better, then that was fine with him.

The miles stretched on, and they had hardly said more than a few words since Ajax had sworn herself to his service. It was flattering really—totally misguided—but flattering. Unless he killed her, he was stuck with a bodyguard. Too bad she wasn't funny. One comedian could scratch out a meager existence by moving from town to town, but two comedians—and one a woman—that would mean even greater benefits.

But in order for them to reap the benefits, she had to have some sort of skill, and based upon their limited conversations, most of which included him trying to make her laugh, Ajax had the sense of humor of a rock.

He broached the idea in the most sensitive way he could think of. "So, uhh, what the hell can you do?"

"Pardon?" She glanced at him out of the corner of her eye, and he sensed something there, something the comedian absolutely hated—pity.

"I mean, I have skills. I'm funny. I can stroll into a town, do my show, and keep myself fed, but usually, I only make enough for myself. So that means if you have no skills, you're probably going to starve to death by the time we get to the next town or the town after."

Ajax chewed on the side of her lip as a four-eared jackrabbit scampered out of their path. Neither of them carried a bow, so it was a missed opportunity to score some meat, although the comedian made it a rule to only eat mutie meat when there was absolutely no other alternative.

"I can kill," she finally said.

The comedian allowed her space to continue, but after four or five dusty steps, he figured out she wasn't going to say anymore.

"You can kill?"

Ajax nodded her head as she pretended to peer off into the distance, although there was nothing to see—hadn't been anything for days.

"Well, you're not funny; we know that."

Ajax harrumphed. "Out of my companions, I was considered the funny one."

The comedian let this news sink in, mentally crumpled it into a ball, and then tossed it into his mind's garbage can. "If you're the funny one, I'm Captain America."

Ajax stopped in her tracks, a perturbed look on her face.

"What?" the comedian asked.

"You are nothing like Captain America."

"Alright, alright, don't get your chainmail in a bunch."

The comedian trudged on, and after a moment, Ajax followed. He was her Broken Man after all.

"So if you're not funny, then can you dance?"

"I can do the dance of death."

"Is that like a sexy dance, or you just spinning around with that mace?"

"It is the dance of life."

"So the dance of death is also the dance of life?" The comedian sucked air through his teeth. "Well, do you do it with your clothes on?"

"I will not whore myself out for beans."

"You say *'for beans.'* Is there something you would uhh—

"No."

"Alright then." The comedian scratched at his head. Inside that head, ideas and thoughts swirled around, floating in a constant lake of subtle, bubbling pain.

Maybe she can do something else physical, Odd chimed in.

The comedian looked down at Oddrey dangling from his chest. Her nose was brown from a small dollop of wetted mud he had placed on the tip to protect her fair skin from burning in the sun. The nose was the most likely part to burn.

Oddrey's words gave him an idea. "Have you ever juggled?"

"Juggled?"

"Don't tell me you don't know what juggling is."

Ajax scoffed at him. "Of course, I know what juggling is. We have many great feats of strength and dexterity on reaping day. Juggling was one of them."

"So you can juggle."

"No. I always participated in the feats of strength."

"Of course you did."

Onward they trudged, the sun beating down upon them, their only relief when burnt, black clouds drifted across the sun, blocking out its burning light.

"You think you can learn?" the comedian asked.

14

"Learn what?"

"To juggle, moron."

"I am not a moron."

Her words were standoffish, and the comedian could tell he'd hurt her pride by the way her lips were pursed. Broken Man or not, it looked to the comedian like she wanted to put him in the dirt. He didn't really care one way or another; it would certainly be an end to all this walking, but on the odd chance they were going to travel together for longer, he thought they needed to clear the air.

"Listen," he began. He trailed off trying to find the right words to make things better, but all that came to mind were jokes and insults. Good stuff, too.

Just tell her who you are, Oddrey said.

"Right. Good idea, Odd." Ajax cocked an eyebrow at this, but the comedian took no notice. "Listen, I'm a bit of an asshole. I don't mean anything by it. I just… I just… I haven't been around a lot of people, and…"

"And you call people names."

"Well, yeah, but I don't mean anything by it!"

"Then why do it?"

"It's banter! That's all! Just banter."

"You banter by insulting?"

"Now you're getting it!"

"You're a stinking poop."

"Yeah. That's it. That's a weird thing to say, but you're getting it."

"You are a broken, sad man with no soul."

"Well, that's a little harsh."

"Your mind is shattered."

"Ok. Enough. It's only banter if it's not true."

"You mean a lie?"

"Kinda."

Ajax fell silent, her hand instinctively going to her mace. The comedian noticed it did this whenever she was uncomfortable, as if she were ready to wreck the world, to batter it into conformity with her own understanding of how it should work.

"I do not lie."

"Ever?"

"Lying is a gateway behavior. First you lie, then you cheat, then you steal, then you are a raider. Everyone knows this."

The comedian rolled his eyes. "Look at me! I lie all the time. Am I a raider?"

"You're worse."

"Pshaw! That right there is a lie!"

Ajax shrugged her shoulders.

"I know you don't think I'm worse than a raider!"

"It remains to be seen."

In silence, they walked, the sky turning orange and bathing them in its waning rays. They picked a spot on a hill overlooking the blasted wastes to make their camp, a defensible spot with good sightlines. As the sun went down, they scrounged bits of desiccated, dry wood, the remains of plants destroyed in the fires of a dying world and suffocated by the blanket of a nuclear winter. As they burned the bones of the old world, they huddled around the fire. The nights in the wastes were cold—could suck the heat right out of you. Fire was a necessity. Fire was life.

The comedian reached into one of the many pockets on his jacket, and produced three rubber balls. He squeezed them for a few minutes, and when the fire crackled and the flames were bright enough, he tossed them to Ajax.

"Here."

Ajax caught them in mid-air, a good sign.

"What do I want with these?"

"You need to learn to juggle."

She tossed the balls back to him. "I am not a performer."

"That's the problem."

16

The stupefied look on Ajax's face made insults bubble up in the back of his throat, but he choked them down, tried to talk to Ajax like he would a daughter... no, not a daughter. Panic welled in his chest as the word zipped across his mind, and he squeezed the rubber balls tight in his hands, forcing the memories away. He didn't need memories now, didn't want them. *Like a child. Yeah, that's the ticket, like a child completely unrelated to you and still alive.*

With a bit of a hitch in his voice, he moved on, lest his emotions get the better of him. "You see, this place we're going, this Ike, if it's like any other town, they're not going to let us in. We are strangers, wasters, untrustworthy scum."

"I am not untrustworthy scum."

"But they don't know that. You go rolling up there like the fucking terminator with your doorknob stick and start banging on the gate, and they're just going to ignore you, maybe put an arrow in your ass."

"I am a Chicken Kicker. We are welcome everywhere where there are good people."

The comedian ran one of his fingerless gloves across his face, the leather rasping across the stubble on his cheeks. *I need to shave before Ike. A shaved face is a trustworthy face.* Plus, it would make him look younger. Last time he'd caught sight of his own reflection, he'd noticed quite a bit more salt in his pepper.

"You there?" Ajax asked.

"Oh. Yeah."

You were talking about Ike, Oddrey said.

"These people are out in the wastes. You've seen the shit out here. They're not going to open the door no matter what type of bird you kick, chicken, swan, duck, pigeon. All they're going to see is someone with a big old doorknob stick."

"It's a mace."

17

"Yeah, yeah. Fact is, you have to make yourself seem like someone they want—no—need to see. That means you have to have skills. See, you said it yourself, Chicken Kickers don't go into the wastes, right?"

"Yes."

"So you're going to need another ticket to the show. And the best way to get into a show is to be a part of it."

The comedian tossed the rubber balls at Ajax, each one thumping gently off her forehead and falling into her lap.

In the glow of the firelight, she looked down at them dubiously.

"That means, you're going to be the juggler."

"The juggler," she said, lost in thought.

"Oh, my god, it's just juggling."

Tentatively, Ajax tossed one of the balls in the air and caught in her hand.

"See? You're a natural."

But she wasn't. Over the course of the next hour, he tried to stifle his laughter as she tried to figure out the trick of juggling.

She has the hand coordination of five-thumbed mutie, Oddrey said.

The comedian kept quiet, though he placed his hand over his mouth, pretending like he was lost in thought. The laughter bubbled up inside threatening to burst from his lips.

You think this is the first time she's ever held balls? Oddrey asked.

"Oh, definitely," he whispered.

Ajax snapped her head in his direction, her eyebrows drawn down and her jaw tight with frustration. "What was that?" she snapped.

"Oh, nothing," the comedian said, barely containing his laughter.

18

The comedian rolled over onto his side, facing away from Ajax so his words wouldn't carry to her. What he had to say was for Oddrey's ears alone.

You could teach her, Oddrey said.

"I could try and teach a dog to ride a bike too, but some things are just impossible." He smiled in the night, looking out over the desolate wastes, lit by the green radglow of the sky.

What are you smiling about then?

"She may not be a juggler, but she can definitely be a fool."

"What are you whispering over there?" Ajax snapped, annoyance apparent in her tone.

The comedian, giddy with hilarity let a small "nothing" escape his lips, and then chomped down on the leather-sheathed palm of his gloved hand to keep his laughter from escaping.

Odd, however, had no such ability to stifle herself, and the comedian fell asleep to her cackling in the night. He loved when Odd laughed. It was the best.

****

From the corner of her eye, Ajax saw the Broken Man roll over on his side and turn his back to her. She knew by the subtle movements of his body he was conversing with the doll head on his chest. Though she knew of his conversations with the doll head, he still tried to hide it, tried to pretend he wasn't broken. In those deceptive leanings, she knew he teetered on the edge, but his attempt to hide his mental state from her gave her hope—far more hope than she had of ever being a juggler.

She snatched the rubber balls off the ground. Pink, yellow, and blue, the balls were not a matched set. The pink ball was bigger than the others, a seam protruding from its side, imperfect, annoying—like the Broken Man. She

19

wanted to take the pink ball and run it through the harsh soil of the wastes, sand that lump right off, but it wasn't her ball, so she didn't.

Taking a deep breath to calm her frazzled mind, she launched the pink ball into the air, then the yellow, then the blue. For a brief moment, she caught the knack of juggling, and then her mind intruded once more as she tried to predict the arcs and flights of the balls. The pink ball dropped to the ground, and she heard the faint stifled laughter of the comedian on the other side of the campfire.

Her face flushed red, and she resisted the urge to pelt the comedian with his own balls. Instead, she snatched the rubber orb off the ground. *Why isn't he helping? Surely, he could teach me how to do this faster than I can figure it out on my own.* She came to an annoying thought, one which was supported by the comedian's stifled laughter. *He thinks this is funny.*

As the balls flew through the air, she didn't even notice she had mastered the trick of juggling. She was too angry with the man on the ground and his stupid doll head. But then as time passed, she did notice, and the balls, as if they had a mind of their own, scattered everywhere. She continued on that night, trying to regain the trick of juggling. She refused to retire until the fire burned low, and the color of the balls faded to shadows. When she could no longer see what she was doing, she laid down to sleep, placing the balls in her satchel for safekeeping. She fell asleep to the tortured murmurings of the comedian and the low sound of dying coals.

****

The next morning brought much of the same—an energy sapping sun, miles of soil that puffed into the air when stepped upon, and many uncomfortable silences.

Onward they trudged, wondering when they would see the town of Ike, whatever the hell that was.

The skies, oddly clear for once, teemed with tube vultures, mutated versions of their once plain cousins. Their beaks, instead of being pointed and sharp for tearing, were rounded. When they found prey, they would insert their beaks into the corpse, slurping up nourishment like a bunch of kids at a fifties malt shop.

The comedian was so busy watching them circle above, he failed to notice the first signs of the wastes relenting. Somewhat sunblind after nervously scanning for shriekers among the tube vultures, the comedian lowered his eyes to take in his surroundings. The ground had some personality to it now. Instead of flat nothingness, there was now a sway and dip to the earth. In pockets of shadow among these low hillocks, sparse bits of greenery struggled to beat back the wastes. Life—unseen since his stumble into Beandick Arnold's valley. The comedian took a deep breath; he could almost smell the chlorophyll. The green plants were a fortuitous sign, for if plants could survive, then so could they.

"You got my balls?" the comedian asked, feeling in the mood for a little conversation. Though he found Ajax completely, mind-numbingly boring, like an old ad for a medication you didn't need, he found talking to her loosened his mind, let his wits stretch their muscles per se.

Ajax reached into her pocket and pulled the balls out.

"Did you figure it out last night?" he asked.

"For a moment. Not sure I'll be much help when we get to Ike."

"Even a poor show is still a show," the comedian said. "That's how soap operas stayed on the TV for so long."

"Soap operas?"

21

"You don't know soap operas? How old are you?" The comedian took a good look at Ajax. She didn't seem much younger than him, but this wasn't the first time something he'd said had gone right over her head. At first, he'd just assumed she was dumb, and that may be, but a suspicion had been growing in the back of his mind.

"Thirty-five winters give or take."

The comedian was a little bit older than that, but not much. He'd lost track of the years some time ago, but he certainly didn't feel older than forty. Still, given her age, he would have expected Ajax to know about soap operas.

"You didn't have TV where you grew up?"

"We had TV."

"But no soap operas?"

"We only had what the Fury would play on Friday nights when all the work was done for the week."

"Lemme guess, Marvel movies and Golden Girls."

"There was more than that."

A thought crossed his mind, but he hesitated, nervous to discover the answer. He licked his chapped lips and ran a gloved hand across his chin. Then he spit out his question. "Were you alive before the death of the world?"

"No."

The comedian stopped in his tracks, clouds of dust drifting away.

Ajax, sensing something was amiss, stopped and turned to face him.

"But you're thirty-five."

Ajax nodded.

The comedian's brain hurt. "But... how old do you think I am?"

Ajax sized him up, tilting her head this way and that. "Forty?"

The math didn't add up, and a sharp pain made the comedian squint his eyes shut. "But if you're thirty-five, you should have been alive when the world was still alive."

22

Ajax shrugged. "I wasn't."

The comedian sat in the dust with a thump. "It doesn't make sense."

"What doesn't?"

"I was twenty-five when the world died. Even if you were born when the bombs were launched, you should only be what fourteen, fifteen?"

Ajax graced him with a look he'd seen before, her patented pitying glance for the poor Broken Man. Normally, he just ignored it, but today he wasn't quite in the mood for it. "Alright, you can stop fucking with me. You were alive before the bombs, weren't you?"

Ajax shook her head. "I remember my father talking about the world before from the time I was little. He would talk about the aeroplanes and the automobiles, the Internet, the library, all those things I had never seen or heard of. When I was a child, I thought he was just making things up. Surely nothing so fantastic as a building filled only with books could be real. By then, the old world was so far gone, I couldn't believe half his tales. Only when I got to The Coop and saw the Fury's movies did I understand his stories weren't stories, but memories."

The comedian dusted off his pants and stood up, a fire lit under his heels. "Bullshit."

He marched on, kicking up puffs of dust, the handle of his massive sword swinging back and forth as he strode up a small hillock. "Major bullshit."

Poppycock, Oddrey echoed.

Ajax pulled her hood over her head and followed along, listening to the comedian's ramblings.

"A bull made out of shit," the comedian called as he descended another hillock, stepping around the sparse bits of greenery living in the shade of the hill. "If you were born after the blasts, then I'm like sixty years old. Do I look sixty to you?" The comedian spun, pulling his goggles from his eyes so Ajax could get a good look at his face.

"No."

"Right." The comedian pulled his goggles back down with certainty. "So either you're lying, or you're shit at math. Which is it?"

"Well, I am not a mathetist if that's what you're asking."

"Mathematician," the comedian corrected.

"We call them mathetists where I come from. It's easier to say."

"That's the problem with the world! Everyone wants to do things the easy way, not the right way. It's math-muh-fuckin'-tician, and don't you forget it. Regardless, I don't think you know when you were born. You must be like twenty. The wasteland ages people. Yeah. That's what's going on. You can't add for shit, the wasteland aged you. Now it all adds up. And that's math, lady!"

Ajax could sense the comedian's agitation, sense he was on the verge of an explosion, so she let him continue with his theories, his wild ramblings, his profuse and copious usage of swearwords. Although in the back of her mind, she had a thought about what had happened. It was time again, breaking down, just as the dying earth opened up with gaping, bottomless wounds, just as the skies burned their bodies with its horrid, sickly light. Time itself was after them, circling like a pack of wolves hunting a lone warrior in the woods, waiting to pounce. Travel together and hold the wolves at bay. Travel on your own, as the comedian had been doing for years, and time pounced, wrapping its foaming muzzle around your ankle and dragging you into the future, or into the past. Ajax might not be a mathetist, but she knew how old she was, could count all of the Coop's harvest festivals up one by one based upon who she had been crushing on that year. There were a lot of crushes.

As they topped the next hillock, standing amongst a patch of swaying green grasses, Ajax looked off into the distance. Through the burnt haze of the wastes, she thought she could see something square and blocky jutting into the sky. She placed a hand to her eyes and squinted, but it could just be a trick of her eyes or of the world. Who knew what the world got up to these days?

"What other words do you bastards shorten in The Coop. Do you call your chainmail chail? What about your mace? Is that just a ma?"

"My mace is called the Holiest of Holys."

A sudden honk of laughter made Ajax forget about the object in the distance, if it was even there at all. When she turned to regard the comedian, he stood doubled over, his hands on his knees and his brown face turning red as he shook with laughter.

"What?"

"What's the name of your mace again?"

"The Holiest of Holys," Ajax said.

Her reply set off another round of laughter from the comedian. Tears welled in his eyes, and he pumped his arms in the air as if combatting invisible demons, perhaps the ones who had taken over his body and forced him to laugh.

"Oh, Jesus. That's rich."

Ajax, at first slightly bemused, grew annoyed. "What? It's a holy mace, the most holiest according to Doctor Weird."

The comedian couldn't stop giggling. "Doctor Weird?" More laughter erupted from the comedian. "What happened to Doctor Strange?"

"He died in a Quidditch match."

The comedian fell over on his side, strands of grass caressing his cheeks as he kicked his feet in the dirt.

"Stop!" he gasped.

Ajax's hand reached for the Holiest of Holys, but then something besides the comedian's boisterous laughter reached her ears.

25

"What's that?"

"The Holiest of Holys!" the comedian replied.

"Silence!" Ajax commanded.

Her tone must have reached something in the comedian, that over-developed part of his brain dedicated to survival. Lying on the ground, his eyes went wide behind his goggles as the sound of rumbling reached his ears. "Oh, shit."

"What is it?" Ajax asked.

"Don't know, but it's coming this way." The comedian popped to his feet, not even bothering to dust himself off. He climbed to the top of the nearest hillock and scanned for the source of the noise, Ajax on his heels. "No, no, no."

"What is it?" Ajax asked.

"Nothing good. You ready to run?"

"I can."

"Well, you fucking well better. Sounds like footsteps, and a lot of them." With that the comedian turned and ran, spitting out one last phrase before he saved his breath for running. "Holiest of Holys," he muttered to his own amusement. Then his arms and legs were pumping, and Ajax rushed to catch up with him.

****

The comedian knew when danger approached. Anything making that much noise was not afraid of what the wasteland had to offer, and that meant they should be very afraid. This was an all or nothing run, the type of run where, if you fell, you just kept rolling until you could get your feet under you because you knew every second meant the source of the sound was getting closer.

Up and down hills they ran, the comedian cursing the weight of his sword and all of his gear. Ajax, burdened only by the mace on her hip and the satchel looped over her

26

torso, soon left him in the dust. But he knew it was just a matter of time until they were both caught.

On they ran, the comedian tasting the dust Ajax left in her wake. Her legs, long and strong, made short work of the hills and hummocks. The comedian, shorter, but more powerful, made up ground as they scrambled uphill, only to lose it as Ajax lengthened her stride on the downslopes.

Ten minutes into their run, Ajax pointed into the distance. "There!" she shouted, her breath ragged from exertion.

The comedian looked where she pointed and spotted the corner of a massive square building, the walls a faded blue. In yellow letters, near one of the building's corners, the word "Ike" was spelled out.

They were almost there. The sight of their destination gifted them both with a spurt of energy, and for the next few minutes, the hills flew by. At the top of one such hill, Ajax turned and looked behind them. When her mouth fell open, the comedian did the same.

"What is that?" Ajax asked.

The comedian, his goggled eyes protected from the glare of the sun, couldn't believe what he was seeing. As the ground shook around them, he caught sight of the source of the earth's quaking in the distance.

"Cats," the comedian said.

Two football fields away, they moved like a giant carpet of fur, leaping and bounding up and over hills, crawling all over each other, their tiny paws pounding the dry earth as they loped along, a tide of fur and claws. They weren't lions or tigers or bobcats, just your ordinary everyday house cats… although, the comedian bet they wouldn't stop to purr and twine around their ankles if they let that feline tide wash over them.

"What do you call that?" Ajax asked.

"It's a bunch of cats. I don't know. But whatever the hell you call it, I think we better not let it catch up to us."

They turned and ran.

I know what to call it. How about a meowl-strom.

"Stop it, Odd."

Ahead, Ajax tossed a disbelieving look over her shoulder, but the comedian paid her no heed. They were running for their lives after all.

A straylude.

Even as he ran, the comedian couldn't hide the smile on his face. A casual observer might think he was grimacing in pain from overexertion, but in reality, Oddrey's list of names for their current predicament went on and on, name after name. If she wasn't so shy, they could clean up with him as the opening act and Odd as the headliner. But she was bashful, kept all of her humor for his ears only.

Furderball.

"That's actually pretty good," he gasped as the faded blue walls of Ike reared up ahead of them, making the survivors feel smaller and smaller the nearer they came. He could see the doors, great glass numbers. The comedian was no mathetist, but he figured if they could hit the doors, open them, and then close them without delay, they might have a chance. Although, if the doors were locked, and Ike was like any other town he had ever visited, they would most likely be forced to wait outside. In that scenario, they would be clawed to death by hundreds of creatures no taller than his shin. *If only I had a ball of string.*

Onward they ran, sweat coursing down their cheeks, the burnt air of the waste never seeming to carry enough oxygen.

Underneath the thunder of thousands of tiny paws battering the wastes, he could hear hissing and caterwauling.

A cat-er-wall, Oddrey said.

And for some reason, at that moment, Odd's joke struck him just right. The comedian began to laugh and run

28

like the madman Ajax so clearly thought he was. Chuckling and gasping for air, they ran onward, hitting the concrete apron that had once surrounded the town of Ike. Instead of cars lined up to shop for affordable, utilitarian furniture, the town of Ike, built inside an old IKEA furniture store, sat lonesome and forlorn on the edge of the wastes.

Ajax and the comedian rushed onward, the comedian laughing insanely. *A cat-er-wall.*

Picking and choosing their way across the jumbled, cracked parking lot, they hurtled toward the glass doors of Ike. The comedian fully intended to hurtle through the glass, but at the last moment, a familiar face made his eyes open wide in shock, and the two companions plunged inside the cool shade of Ike while two wasters in faded yellow t-shirts sealed the glass doors behind them.

A wall of furry death crashed into the glass, and the comedian and Ajax spun to behold their certain doom. But when they turned around, the herd of cats sat on the other side of the glass, cooling themselves in the shade of Ike's walls. They sat on their haunches, cleaning their paws, licking the waste dust off their little toes. Their tales twitched and swirled, and they stared at the two companions, squinting their eyes as if to say, "We'll get you sooner or later."

One of the cats sprayed the glass, and then, as one, they sauntered off, seemingly in no rush at all.

Chapter 2: Ike

"I see you survived the purrthquake," one of the yellow-shirted people said.

Purrthquake! Why didn't I think of that? Oddrey asked.

The comedian turned to the face he had seen as he entered Ike, familiar, fair-eyed, and somewhat sheepish. He locked in on Yokel and said, "What the hell are you doing here? You followin' us?"

"I was here first," Yokel said, cocking a finger at himself.

"Pretty sneaky way to follow someone," the comedian said, squinting his eyes at the diminutive man.

Yokel let his hand drop and the comedian noticed for the first time the shirt he wore. It was a faded blue t-shirt, the words "I like Ike" scrawled across the front in a flowing yellow script.

"Like the shirt, by the way."

Yokel smiled his weird little smile, and the comedian took in his surroundings, aware he was being studied by the yellow-shirted Ikeans. He stood in a courtyard of sorts. Above, bare rafters held up the roof of the building. Among the many struts and pylons moved lanky humans, hopping like monkeys from beam to beam in their excitement. On the ground, the courtyard was cordoned off with piles of cheap but well-made furniture, stacked willy-nilly to create a massive barricade. The plain concrete floor was dotted with a line of yellow arrows leading through an opening in the massive barricade. Other than the Ikeans, there was nothing else in the courtyard.

From the narrow path, a man in a yellow and blue striped robe emerged, bent and stooped. The hood shrouding his face came to a comical point.

"Motherfucker looks like a wizard."

"Magic?" Ajax asked, her tone reverent and curious.

"Magic's not real, ya dingus."

"I am not a dingus."

The other Ikeans backed away, and for the first time, the comedian took note of the weapons on their arms. They looked like the liberated sides of shopping carts, cut into shield shapes, each loose tine on the edge of the shield sharpened to a point that could easily puncture skin. As the Ikean wizard plodded on, the yellow-shirts stood ready and alert as they watched the robed man approach with a reverence that made the comedian's skin crawl.

Worship was for the weak. To hold someone in such high esteem, even if they deserved it, was not in his nature. So when he saw idolatry, he couldn't help but be revolted. However, he was here for a purpose, and that purpose's name was Cheatums Sterling.

The old man, who smelled of must and dust, stopped three feet short of the comedian. "Hey," the man said.

"Hey yourself," the comedian responded.

Ajax held her clasped hands out in front of her, bowed her head and said, "Hey," in an overly respectful tone that caused the comedian's jaw to clench.

Brown-noser, Oddrey said.

Perhaps he was nervous, or perhaps he had been in the wastes too long, but even the presence of other people had his heart thumping in his chest. He stopped short of reaching for Side-Splitter, the massive sword on his back, but somewhere in the back of his mind, he thought this might be the best possible outcome. His sixth sense, long absent in the wastes, was back, and it was telling him to cut everyone down. In his head, within the span of a few heavy heartbeats, he had mapped out a course of brutal action that would leave several Ikeans without their heads and various other body parts.

31

The old man lifted his head to expose a bulbous nose and ruddy, red skin. His eyes were permanently cocked so that one bugged out and the other was almost partially closed. "Welcome to Ike."

"Yeah, great. You got a guy named Cheatums here?" the comedian asked, his palms itching to hold his sword.

"Whoa, whoa, whoa," the man said. "What is the rush? Here we favor the Long Natural Path. Time is the only resource we still have plenty of in this world, so we take advantage of it."

Something clever tingled on the precipice of the comedian's lips, but before that caustic bubble could burst, Ajax stepped in.

"Pardon our rushed ways. We have traveled long and far to reach you. Perhaps we have been in the wastes too long. Perhaps we are still rattled from fleeing from a herd of murderous cats. Either way, we humbly apologize and beg your forgiveness."

The robed man nodded. "Well spoken, and well met kind travelers. It's been a while since I myself have been out of the safety of Ike. Perhaps I would do better to remember the horrors of the wastes."

Ajax cast a triumphant glance in the comedian's direction. For once, he kept his words to himself. If he didn't have to talk, he wouldn't. Instead, he turned his focus inward, preparing himself for the performance. There was always a performance. Sometimes that performance came in the form of comedy. Other times, the performance came in the form of the sword. But there was always a show to put on.

"You mentioned a man's name, a man that's known to us. Cheatums? Yes?"

The comedian nodded.

"We are on a quest to find this man," Ajax said.

"Well, I regret to inform you he has moved on."

Alarm bells rang in the comedian's ears, and he couldn't resist speaking. "Moved on? As in dead?"

The robed man cracked a gentle smile and chuckled a bit. "Oh, no. Pardon my phrasing. He's not here anymore, but last I saw he was quite alive."

"Do you have any idea of where he went?" The comedian was unaware of the desperation in his voice. If he had noticed, he would have hated himself for it, but time was important.

"Come, come, my rushing friend. First, let us eat together and see how we might help each other. The path is long, and rushing to the end only leads to missing out on fine deals."

"Deals?"

"All will be made clear."

The robed man placed a guiding hand on the comedian's shoulder, whose defense mechanisms immediately kicked in. "No touching."

The robed man pulled his hand from the comedian's shoulder, left it hanging in the air in the way of apology. Then he turned, and shouted to the other Ikeans in a voice louder than the comedian would have expected from the shambling, stooped man. "Bulla bulla!" He cupped his hands to his mouth and yelled the nonsensical phrase once more. "Bulla bulla!" The sound of his voice echoed throughout the rafters of the massive warehouse, and all around, the Ikeans picked up the call.

"Bulla bulla!" the rafterpeople shouted as they leapt about the ceiling, swinging from rafter to rafter like acrobats. From the other side of the barricade, answering calls filled the cavernous space of Ike with voices of all pitches and timbres, men's voices, women's voices, and those in between.

From the path between the two barricades, people began to emerge, wasters in appearance, though here and there, another person in a yellow shirt striated with blue

33

would appear. As the comedian tried to put together the rules and culture of Ike, assemble the puzzle of these people, the robed man turned to him, that gentle, old man smile on his face.

"My name is Kallax, Lord of the Wrenches...

Lord of being creepy as fuck, Oddrey said.

"...and I welcome you to Ike." With his last words, he spread his arms wide, as if displaying a massive mound of treasure instead of a group of filthy wasters and furniture the comedian wouldn't have bought back when the world was still alive.

I don't trust these people, Odd whispered.

The comedian just nodded.

Ajax, sensing the comedian was locked in conversation with the doll on his chest, stepped up and said, "My name is Ajax, and this is the comedian."

"He's the one I been tellin' ya about," Yokel added.

Kallax nodded. "Welcome," he said. "We could use some mirth around here."

"Are you in charge?" the comedian asked.

At this, Kallax laughed as he plopped down into a cross-legged position on the cold, gray concrete. "Oh, no. I'm just a co-worker. The regional manager will be along in a bit. But please, sit, so we might talk."

The comedian didn't want to sit. The wasters who had crawled from the rest of the building, like ants from a kicked anthill, had crowded around. They stood, dirty and silent, not the way he was usually greeted. On their faces, he didn't see the signs of distrust, but neither did he see the signs of excitement. Those were the two reactions he usually received whenever he strolled into a town. This silent ogling by their round eyes did nothing to alleviate the persistent itch on the back of his neck. He ran a gloved palm across his nape, but the itch did not relent.

Still, when in Rome. The comedian plopped on the ground, crossing his legs, and unsheathing Side-Splitter so he could sit properly and unleash the fury of the sword if it was required. To his right, Ajax did the same. Sitting across from the Lord of the Wrenches, a silence fell over them. One of the wasters coughed, and Kallax cast a cock-eyed glare in their direction.

Eventually, the comedian tired of the silence and said, "So what now?"

"Now we breathe," Kallax added. "In, as deep as you can, filling your lungs, and out through your nose."

"No, I'm not doing that."

Kallax cocked his head. "You are willful, strong-headed. But of course, you must be to make it all the way out to Ike. It's been a while since we've had visitors such as yourself, and now we've had five in a matter of a week. Truly, the wrenches portend something great happening. Perhaps this is a time of change for Ike."

I don't really give a fuck about Ike. "Perhaps," the comedian managed to say, remembering to play his part. *Read the room, adjust, play the part.*

"You said five people?" Ajax asked.

"Oh, yes. So many guests in such a small amount of time. An amazing development. Why it had been a year since we had any visitors. In fact, we were starting to think we were all alone out here."

"Will you tell us the story of your town?" Ajax asked. "I have never been in so large a building."

Kallax laughed and nodded. "All in due time, but that is not a story for me to tell. That is for the regional manager."

"And where is this regional manager?" the comedian asked.

"He comes... but in the meantime, shall we throw the wrenches?"

The comedian tried to make sense of the phrase, tried to understand why a thrilled gasp went up from the assembled crowd of wasters.

35

Unable to puzzle out the significance of *throwing the wrenches*, the comedian said, "Uh, I'm not sure what you mean. Where I come from, we don't throw wrenches."

Another gasp went up from the crowd, this one full of disbelief.

"I am the Allen. A seer." Kallax opened his robe wide and revealed an array of Allen wrenches suspended within. "With these, I can tell your future."

Another goddamn prophet? Oddrey asked.

Ajax nodded. "The future is a great gift, but we have nothing to offer in kind."

"You come to perform. Your man has told us such."

The comedian glanced at Yokel. The coolant-head turned away and began kicking at an imagined piece of dirt on the concrete floor with the well-worn toe of his shoe.

Annoyed at how the world seemed to be conspiring against him, attaching fools to his hip, the comedian made a counter offer. "A future without food is soon a future unrealized. If I had to choose between a telling of my future, and food and drink, I would choose food and drink every day."

Kallax smiled. "If you are as funny as you are wise, then food and drink and future will be a bargain."

Kallax held out his hand, urging the comedian to strike the deal. The comedian reached out and grasped the man's shaking hand.

He's a cannibal, Oddrey said, as if the comedian couldn't see the signs.

He might be, or he might simply be old as fuck.

"A deal!" Kallax shouted, and the wasters around them burst into raucous cheering. "Bulla bulla!" they screamed.

"What is *bulla bulla?*" Ajax asked.

"It is simply our way. Store secrets you know." The old man tapped a finger against the side of his nose and then rose from his seat in a single spry motion. "Come, we must gather around the arrow of destiny."

Kallax walked across the concrete floor, and the comedian and Ajax followed. Upon reaching one of the yellow arrows that pointed toward the path leading between the barricades, the old man squatted once again. Immediately, the roar of chanting from the Ikeans ceased, their echoes fading among the rafters.

Allen wrenches jingled and jangled as Kallax plucked them from his robe, which upon closer inspection, the comedian could see was an old throw rug, faded and filthy. Once he had liberated all of his wrenches, Kallax began to speak, his eyes rolling into the back of his head.

Out of the corner of his eye, he caught Ajax mouth the word "magic."

Magic my ass. No such thing.

Kallax grabbed the wrenches in his gnarled hands, lifted them in the air and dashed them down on the ground with an ear-splitting clang. The wrenches, of all different sizes, splashed this way and that, clanging all about. When they had settled, Kallax leaned forward so his face was parallel with the ground, and only his bulbous nose peeked out from underneath his fringed hood. The Ikeans "oohed" and "aahed" as he made a great show of studying the wrenches.

In his mind, the comedian imagined making a jacking off gesture. He prevented his eyes from rolling in his head which became even harder after he glanced over at the rapt face of Ajax. *Magic. Psshh.*

The people in the rafters hung precariously from the beams as they took in the scene.

Then Kallax, with a showmanship the comedian couldn't help but admire, leaned back, his eyes closed and his right hand held out before him, palm flat, fingers pointing to the ceiling. Thus, he intoned his prophecy. "Silver, I see silver in your future, and blood. A fellowship, unwanted but necessary, shall be built. The sins of the past shall present themselves once more and good will be the cost of your salvation. Some may perish, and the one may be broken so that the many may flourish, or perhaps it is the other way around. The wrenches are not clear on this point. Your footsteps bring loss, but it is up to you to decide if that loss has any meaning. Everywhere you go, blood and fire."

The robed man's warbling voice trailed off. "Also, there's a shitload of walking."

The comedian listened half-heartedly, only putting on a show of listening. *Prophecies. Magic.* These things were fictions. Just as the religions of the past had been used to salve the conscience of the masses for millennia, so too was the newfound wasteland belief in magic and prophecies.

What about the ramen shaman? Or Beandick? They were magic, Oddrey chimed in.

Hokum.

Then how do you explain it?

My brain's busted.

Both things can be true, magic and busted brains.

Hokum, the comedian thought, dismissing Oddrey's line of thinking. As he did, the robed man wound down, his body shrinking in upon itself, his back turning crooked once more as he stooped.

"He comes," the Ikeans whispered, shushed and reverent, and slightly fearful. From the path between the barricades, a man emerged, his skin dark, his head bald, his eyes bugging out. Clad in another of those yellow shirts with the blue stripes, the only thing marking him as different from the others was a lanyard hanging around his neck, a card that read "Manager" prominently displayed. A hush fell over the crowd once more, and the comedian sensed something else besides reverence for the leader of

38

this settlement. He sensed apprehension. Indeed, his own sixth-sense began to act up.

"Hey," the manager said to them. Kallax, the robed man, shuffled off to the side and bowed deferentially to his superior.

"Howdy," the comedian said back, executing a bow so perfect, and so theatrical, the crowd couldn't help but murmur in appreciation, remarking upon his grace. *It's time to start the show.*

"You must have traveled a long way to get here. Come, you must be tired." The manager clapped his hands and the wasters surged into action, selecting furniture from the barricades, hustling like ants carrying pieces of leaves they had cut with their mandibles. All around them, the wasters streamed and swarmed while the comedian held still, perfectly still, waiting for the attack to come.

Instead, within a matter of seconds, an entire living room had appeared around them. The regional manager bade them to sit on a couch as he lowered himself onto its mirror image. The wasters backed away, their heads bowed, and the comedian knew this place was fucked. Something in the eyes of the wasters, in the lusty anticipation of the people in the rafters.

The manager leaned back, throwing an arm over the back of the couch as he crossed his legs which were clad in faded dress pants, often mended. The dress shoes on his feet showed their wear. A hole in one of the soles made the comedian feel uncomfortable. This was a man who did not run. Everyone in the wasteland knew proper footwear was of the utmost importance. While this man might be putting on a show of civility now, the fact that he, as the leader, would wear such impractical footwear told the comedian much. First, he was in charge, totally and completely. Second, he never ventured outside of the walls of Ike. Third, he was probably a dangerous, despotic lunatic. One did not wield the control this man had on charm and good looks alone, and as far as the comedian could tell, this man had neither charm nor good looks.

"Tell us," the manager said, the very picture of casual, "how did you get here?"

The comedian, in no mood for storytelling, just wanted to know where Cheatums was hiding. He was about to speak, when Ajax laid a hand on his arm. From there, she began their tale, leaving out the good parts, all the killing of raiders and the comedian's frequent jokes and hilarity. Her story was boring, profoundly so, but it afforded him the opportunity to study the crowd around them. The wasters yawned as Ajax spun her yarn with all the proficiency of a five-year-old describing a dream.

"…and then there was a crone, and she said…"

The bodies of the wasters were thin and emaciated, their arms, legs, and torsos covered with grit and grime as if they had been rolling in mud for most of their lives. Most of them stood almost bare-assed naked but for scraps of clothing held together with zip ties and poor stitching. Dotted among these pitiful examples of humanity stood the yellow-shirted middle class. They were clean by wasteland standards, their flesh more filled out than the others. They stood with an air of confidence that came with higher social standing. As the manager listened to their story, so too did the yellow shirts. Meanwhile, the wasters cast their eyes at the yellow shirts every so often, as if awaiting a signal. *Things could go very badly, very quickly here.*

Above, the rafter people stared down at them. As the comedian leaned his head back and studied them, he noted that most of them were young, in their teens. They glared down at the people below with the cocksure intensity of adolescence. They weren't the only things in the rafters. As he studied the ceiling, Ajax droning on and on, he saw piles of cables attached at various points among the beams, for descending he supposed.

"So, a quest, is it?" the regional manager intoned.

40

"Yes, a quest," Ajax said.

"Noble indeed."

"So, you seen Cheatums or what?" the comedian asked.

A lone gasp went up from the crowd, someone mortified at the comedian's adroitness with the regional manager. The manager played his part, maintaining the yellow-toothed smile on his face, even as his arm slid from the back of the couch. He leaned forward and steepled his hands together, chopping at his lips with his fingertips, lost in thought. "Yes, we have seen this Cheatums."

The comedian felt a small glimmer of hope. Maybe for once, things were going to be easy. Maybe, just this one time, someone would give him exactly what he wanted without making him jump through hoops, maybe...

"But you see, Co-worker Cheatums has decided to join our lovely operation. He has begun his journey into the inner sanctum. He has taken the Long Natural Path."

Fuck. Nothing was ever easy. "Well, bring him back," the comedian said, as if it were the most obvious solution in the world.

The manager spread his hands wide, as if to say there was nothing he could do. "Once one begins the Long Natural Path, there is no coming back until the path is completed."

"How long will that take?" Ajax asked.

"It's different for all those who undertake it. The path is a test of sorts of strength and will. Those who succeed are welcomed whole-heartedly into the fold. Those who fail... well, death is the most likely outcome."

"Can we take this path?" the comedian asked.

The regional manager smiled at them. The sunlight filtering in through the glass doors reflected off his lemon-colored choppers, making them glow. "I'm sorry. We have no openings at this time. But should Co-worker Cheatums not complete the path, I would be more than happy to interview you, for then we would have an opening."

The comedian ran the situation through his mind. "So lemme get this straight. Cheatums is somewhere where we can't go, and he may or may not die."

The manager nodded his head.

"We can't talk to him because you're full up on staff."

The manager nodded once more. His smile would be disarming, if it wasn't for the sadistic glint in his eye.

"And the only way we can take the path is if he dies, at which point, it would be totally unnecessary because the man I need to talk to is dead."

The manager nodded his head once more. "You have the right of it. I kinda wished you had showed up a few days earlier. You seem like you would make a much more versatile employee than Co-worker Cheatums."

Ajax sighed. "I guess all we can do is wait."

The manager leaned forward once more, his fingers steepled in front of his mouth like a chess master planning out his next move. "There is something you can do for me while we wait."

The comedian only half listened. "It's gonna be a quest," he muttered to himself.

The manager, undeterred by the comedian's comment, plowed ahead. "There is an item I need recovered, something of great importance to me. You see, the reason we have an opening now is that one of our Co-workers has fled to our competitor."

"What is this item?" Ajax asked.

The comedian thought she was getting off on the idea of a quest. As for the comedian, he was tired of them. Tired of doing the fetching and fighting others were too lazy or too weak to do on their own.

The manager described the item to them, a silver brick, twelve-inches long. When he was finished, the manager slapped the thighs of his ancient dress pants and stood. "But first, I believe, according to your good man, you have a show to share with us, yes?"

The comedian nodded. "We pay our own way."

"Good," the manager said. "Life can get pretty drab around here. I'm sure your performance will go a long way toward boosting team morale. In repayment, we shall supply you, should you decide you will undertake the task I have set before you."

The comedian was about to tell the man to go fuck himself, when Ajax spoke up. "We'll do it."

"Fantastic. Well, I would love to stick around for the show, but I have some paperwork to do." With that, the manager clapped his hands, and the wasters swooped in, literally pulling the couch out from under the comedian and Ajax. They whirled and danced quickly, the living room disappearing as if it never existed. The swirl of bodies around the comedian had him on edge, and when the flurry of activity stopped, the manager was gone.

Kallax, the robed man, hobbled in their direction. "What is it you need for your show?"

The comedian, locked into a course of action thanks to Ajax's big mouth, said, "A stage, something to string my lights from."

Kallax nodded and called over a few yellow shirts. He gave them directions, and then the yellow shirts turned to the wasters, setting off another flurry of activity. While this was going on, the comedian pulled Ajax to the side to plan for the show. But before that, he laid into her a little bit.

"Don't ever speak for me."

"What?"

"I mean this quest. It's a waste of time. A waste of resources. I am no one's errand boy. We're already in here, and these people... well, let's just say, we could have taken what we wanted."

"At what cost?"

"Cost. Pshh. A few dead wasters, but only the ones who got in our way. What's wrong with that?"

"You're worse than a raider."

"Take it back."

"To take back the truth is tantamount to lying."

"God, I hate you."

"The feeling is mutual."

"Then go. Leave. I don't need you."

"My quest is not yet complete. The Broken Man shall be mended."

The comedian could only grunt his frustration.

"I can help," a voice said, startling the comedian.

"Jesus!" the comedian cried. "When the hell did you get here?" Until Yokel had spoken, he hadn't even known he was there, even though he was hard to miss in his blue "I like Ike" T-shirt.

"You can help by staying out of the way."

"But, I have skills."

"Listen, radiator cocktails are great and all, but I wouldn't necessarily call it a skill."

"No, I am a cinematist."

"I don't see a projector," the comedian said, making a show of studying Yokel and looking behind him.

"No, a cinematist doesn't show movies. They tell movies."

"That's stupid as fuck," the comedian said.

Ajax chimed in. "I have seen cinematists before. They travel like you, and are welcome all over. Children especially love the work of the cinematist. It could be worth something to these people."

The comedian considered it, and then realized his opening act was a bumbling mess who would likely elicit nothing more than a few derisive sniggers. Also, it would give him more time to tailor his show. He had studied the people enough to have a few ideas, but nothing solid. He needed a distraction. "Alright, you get one audition, but you fuck it up, and that's it."

Yokel pumped his fist, and then spun in a circle, his hands in the air. "I made it. The big time."

"Yeah, yeah. Just get your movie picked out."

Yokel stood off to the side, near the front doors of Ike, his hands and lips moving as he practiced the movie he would tell. The comedian pulled Ajax to the side, produced the balls from his jacket, and handed them over. "Here. Now, it's going to be rough for you up there, but whatever happens don't get flustered. Smile like it's all a joke, even if you fuck up. You're the opener, then the cinematist, whatever the fuck that is, and I'll close it all out."

"I'm nervous," Ajax said.

"You should be. You kind of suck."

Her face turned red, and the comedian stalked away.

That was mean, Oddrey said.

"She's the one that's all about the truth. I'm just following her lead."

You enjoyed it.

"It's the little things, Odd. The little things."

Chapter 3: T.C.'s Carnival of Curiosities

When the platform was constructed and the comedian had strung his lights about, Yokel climbed the steps leading to the center of the stage. It was the largest stage the comedian had ever performed on. Real estate in wasteland settlements was a precious commodity. The more stuff in your city, the longer your walls, the more people you needed to guard the place, so most stages he performed on had the footprint of a postage stamp.

Yokel bowed his head in the silence as the wasters sat looking on, their elbows resting on their filth-slathered knees. The comedian, standing off to the side, waiting for his cue, studied the audience, sensed their reluctance to engage. They were what people in the industry would refer to as a "cold" audience. Their faces hung somber, their everyday worries still present and weighing them down. This was the type of audience that had necessitated the invention of the two-drink minimum in most comedy clubs. A little lubrication in the form of alcohol, and your audience would warm right up. But alcohol was in short supply these days, and the homemade stuff was likely to turn you blind as well as drunk. Maybe having Yokel as a hype man wasn't such a bad idea after all.

"Ladies and gentleman, and all those in-between, welcome to T.C.'s Carnival of Curiosities. Tonight, we have a very special show. For the first time ever, we present Ajax. Capable of rare feats of agility and dexterous daring-do, prepare to have your mind blown as she shows off her superhuman nimble-osity."

The comedian shrugged. *Not bad.*

He's gotten better, Oddrey said.

"After that, I, Yokel, the premiere cinematist of our age, shall tell you a tale so horrid, so wretched, you'll throw up in your own lap and thank me for it!"

"I change my mind," the comedian muttered.

The crowd seems to like it.

Indeed they did. Where before their faces had been locked in abject passivity, now their eyes were wide. Many of the people sitting on their rear ends leaned forward, hanging on Yokel's every word. In the beams above, the rafterpeople hung from struts, their legs swinging in the air, trying to lean closer to the stage to hear every word.

"But wait! There's more!" Yokel intoned. "After I have wowed you with my tales of dark depravity, along comes the grand finale—the comedian! You'll laugh so hard, you'll soil your breeches, if you're wearing any!" Yokel pointed at a loinclothed man, who nodded and laughed.

"It'll just go on the floor!" the man guffawed, and the other filthy wasters around him nodded their heads, as if they had seen it all before. The yellow shirts cast an annoyed look at the waster, and the comedian figured somewhere down the line, he would pay for his comment. But for now, the yellow shirts let him be, though their jaws clenched, and they gripped the handles of their shopping cart shields tighter in their hands.

"The price of all this? Absolutely nothing. If you ain't got nothin', you owe us nothin'. But if you do have something to give, we would appreciate it, as it'll help us get to the next town where we might relieve the tedium and dread of this world. No donation is too small, and certainly none is too large! So, now, without further ado, making her debut with T.C.'s Carnival of Curiosities, Ajax!"

The audience, caught up in the showmanship of Yokel, gave Ajax a nice round of applause, and the comedian winced as she edged out onto the stage, side-stepping along it as if she expected to be shot with an arrow at any point.

The audience fell quiet, their exuberance fading to mild disinterest. As Ajax neared the middle of the stage, her face bright red and a faint tremor in her legs, she produced the comedian's balls, and set about spinning them in a circle.

"Aw, byoo! I can do that!" one of the audience members yelled.

"You calls that jugglin'?" a one-eyed man asked. "Try holding ten hex bolts and an Allen wrench in your hand while trying to put together a Baggebo bookcase with a yellow shirt looking over ya shoulda!"

The other wasters laughed at the man, a righteous chuckle, and then one of the yellow shirts moved to stand behind him, and his mirth dried up.

On stage, Ajax grimaced as she concentrated on keeping the balls in the air, which so far, she had done. But it was only a matter of time now.

The comedian scanned the audience reading their abject boredom, all except for one woman who locked eyes with the comedian. She was rail-thin, covered in more grease and filth than the undercarriage of a garbage truck, and when he locked eyes with her, she licked her lips suggestively.

The comedian pretended not to see her, and let his eyes scan over the rest of the audience.

Ooh. You got a fan, Oddrey said.

Through his smile, he quietly mouthed the words, "Not interested."

Who can resist those greasy charms? Teeth like corn. Hair like what one might find in the shower drain of a radiation triage center.

"Cut it out, Odd."

Ajax's performance sucked the life out of Ike. In truth, he had expected her to fuck up before now. That she

48

had been able to keep juggling the balls for how long she had was commendable—completely not what he wanted, but commendable. It was time to take action.

Placing his hand over his mouth to disguise his voice, he yelled sharply, "You suck, Ajax!" Immediately, her concentration broke, and one of the balls dropped to the ground, bounced, and tumbled off-stage. Ajax stood like a mutated elk caught in the glare of an evercrack, her eyes wide and large. Her face turned the delightful shade of strawberry milk. She made no move to retrieve the ball. In fact, it was as if the possibility of failing had never entered her mind, and she had no clue what to do next. The comedian reached into his bag and plucked out his potential final meal, a half-eaten pomato Ajax had brought from Beandick Arnold's protected patch of paradise. He hefted it in his hand, winked at Ol' Greasy who had been watching him in the audience, and then chucked the pomato at Ajax.

She ducked the fruitable, spinning on stage, and the crowd oohed and aahed, marveling at her alacrity. This was, of course, great fun for the audience. In the comedian's mind, he started thinking up names for Ajax's act, even as random items flew through the air.

The Human Target, Oddrey chimed in.

"I like it."

On-stage, Ajax ducked, dived, and dipped, dodging all of the items thrown her way, bits of filthy cloth, Allen wrenches, hex bolts, scraps of food. Not much on their own, but they were a bevy of riches when all added up. They were getting rich off this.

The blue ball Ajax had dropped, rolled its way to his foot, and he picked it up off the ground, gave it a little squeeze, and then hucked it at Ajax as hard as he could. It thonked off her forehead, and she shot him an imperious glare. The comedian shrugged his shoulders and shot her his winning smile. As the rain of items slackened, Ajax stood on stage fuming.

Sensing a potential calamity, the comedian hopped on stage. "Ladies and gentlemen, and all those in-between, how 'bout a round of applause for... The Human Target!"

The crowd erupted in a rowdy cheer, and the anger melted from Ajax's face. A small smile—a quirky thing out of place on her normally stoic face—made its way to her lips, like the brief glimpse of the sun on a cloudy morning.

"Take a bow," the comedian whispered to her from the side of his mouth.

This she did to more applause. Then she did it again, and the comedian said, "Get off the stage, dingus."

Basking in their adulation, Ajax scooted sideways across the stage, the quirky smile growing bigger and bigger. The comedian pretended to kick at her as she left the stage and the audience died down.

"And now, our next amazing act, you've seen him around here for quite a while. He likes Ike, and you'll love him. It's Yokel, the cinematist!"

Yokel came bounding on stage, his arms spread wide. The crowd waited intently, and the comedian gave up the stage to the odd little man.

Where does he get those shirts? Oddrey asked.

"Who cares. Let's see how he does."

The comedian gave Ajax a friendly slap on the shoulder as he came to stand next to her. "Nice work," he managed to mutter. Ajax didn't reply, and her eyes burned into him, but that smile stayed glued to her face as Yokel began to work his magic.

"Picture this," Yokel began. "A hitchhiker, clad in blue, sexy spandex waits upon the side of a dusty, rocky road. Suddenly, a yuppie, a sort of rich capitalist with no morals, comes speeding around the corner..."

Yokel spun his yarn, describing a film as bizarre as it was entertaining. He told the tale of a hard rock band lured to a small town, whereupon the band was killed because the town was against "rock music." From there, using something called the "bass-riff of resurrection," the band rose from the grave to take their revenge on Hitler, the crazed hitchhiker, a couple of dwarf fiends, and a werewolf Eva Braun, only to return to their grave once more, having saved the world from doom.

The comedian didn't know if what Yokel described was a real movie or not, and he bet that if it were a real movie, it wouldn't be one he wanted to watch. But the way Yokel told it, with the fervor of an oracle, made the comedian imagine every wretched scene. As if in a trance, Yokel wove a world from the past, a horrible world, a cheesy world, but a world every single member of the audience would trade up for in a heartbeat. He filled their chests with longing for things like cars, rock music, naked hitchhikers with clean teeth and no rad lesions. He made them dream of the times that came before, of the glories humanity had built upon this planet. In the end, that was the goal of a cinematist, to bring the old world alive and wipe away the horrors of today.

Yokel's retelling of *Hard Rock Zombies* was so glorious that a small pinprick of pain blossomed in the comedian's heart, and if you could open his chest and peer at that pinprick, you would find a window to a world long gone, one never to return. A world where people did shit like mow their lawns, or watch catty basketball wives bust each other's balls on faux-reality TV. You'd find a world where people bickered over what the laws should be, arguing over which rich capitalist should decide the laws every regular person should live by. It wasn't a perfect world, but it was a damn sight better than what they had now. Even living in a world where smalltown folk killed rock bands because they were tools of the devil would be preferable to the comedian's world. At least those townsfolk had a reason. In this world, some people would kill you for no reason at all.

51

As Yokel started retelling the credits for the film, the comedian broke out of his reverie, cleared his throat loudly, and twirled his finger in the air, signifying to Yokel to get on with it.

"Uh, uh," he stammered.

"Who the hell memorizes credits?" the comedian murmured.

Who the hell watches movies like that? Oddrey added.

The comedian shrugged, and then after Yokel's introduction, he bounded on the stage, his jacket left safely bundled near Ajax's boots. The shirt he wore underneath gleamed brightly, oddly clean after a week in the wastes and a few days spent in a place called Shithole. It glowed with cleanliness despite the dim interior of Ike. A khaki drab, the comedian's shirt was another tool, a sign of order and warmth designed to evoke memories of nostalgia.

In his hands, he held Side-Splitter. He raised the sword in the air, and then drove it downward, impaling it in the back of one of the bookcases serving as a stage. It wavered and wobbled for a moment, and then the comedian leaned forward, clicked a switch on the hilt and bathed himself in the lights built into the sword's crossbar. With a flick of his wrist, he pulled the handle/microphone free.

Looking out onto the audience, he devoured their anticipation, ate it up greedily. There was nothing better than being onstage, no place more sacred. Here he could go anywhere, transport himself back in time if he wanted to or air his grievances with the state of the world. Out of the corner of his eye, he saw his own personal God appear. Short, curly-haired, and just about the funniest person who had ever walked the planet, the comedian didn't know if he was crazy or if the spirit of Pauly Shore was really standing there. Either way, Pauly gave him a nod, and he knew he was blessed one way or another.

Break a leg, buuuuuuuuuuuddy!

The comedian stood ready.

"Good evening, Ike!" The comedian rambled across the luxurious space of the stage, making eye contact with the audience, connecting ocularly with as many people as possible. In a comedy show, it wasn't only the comedian who put on a performance. If you made eye contact with the audience members, they felt like they were seen, and once they felt like the comedian was watching them, they would put on their own show of laughs and smiles for the comedian's benefit. "It's a pleasure to be here. You know, I've been to a lot of places, but none have shown me the hospitality you guys have. You don't usually see that in other places in the wasteland. Most places you have to answer questions or go on a quest to even get in the gates. But not here. So thank you for your hospitality.

"Now that there's like no jobs or anything, going to a new town is the closest we get to having to do job interviews. You remember that bullshit? Getting all dressed up, putting on your best clothes, which you won't wear again for like another year. Hell, now no one even has 'best clothes'. It's not like this dude," he said, pointing at a near-naked waster, "has a chest of drawers back there where he keeps his clean loincloth. Am I right?"

The waster in the audience nodded his head while his buddies slapped him on the shoulders.

"Job interviews were the worst. There you are sitting across from some jerkoff who holds all the power. You're uncomfortable, nervous, trying to read this fucker's mind while they begin peppering you with questions. Meanwhile, you're lying through your teeth the whole damn time. What's your greatness weakness? Uh... I work too hard. Yeah, that's it. Never taken a day off in my life. Meanwhile, you were fired from your last gig at the Vienna sausage plant because you kept calling in sick every time they scheduled you to work on a Sunday during football season.

"Why do you want to work here? You say, 'Because I really admire your company and I want to be a part of the team.' Really what you wanna say is, 'Because I have fucking bills to pay and this looks like the least worst place imaginable for me to work. Plus, the titty bar down the street wasn't hiring dressing room attendants.'

"'Have you ever stolen from a place that you worked?' they ask. Wouldn't it be nice to say, 'Hell, yeah. I've stolen pizza, soda, paint, mineral spirits, beer, and maybe a set of Allen wrenches or two.'"

Instead of a laugh, the audience gasped at his blasphemy, and the comedian knew he'd read them wrong. In full "damage control" mode, he plowed ahead, switching gears. "Now, when you go to some other town, it's the same thing, only the questions are a little different. Instead of asking if you steal things, they're all, 'Are you a cannibal?' No, sir I am not. Never ate even the slightest bit of human meat. This dude stares at you, trying to detect if you're lying or not, even though you both know you are, then finally, if you do it right, you both pretend like you were telling the truth. Instead of asking, are you a good co-worker, they ask you how many people you've killed. And you can never tell the truth. You can't be all, 'Sixty-five. I've killed sixty-five humans. Mostly bare-butt raiders.' They're not gonna let you in with that. Sixty-five people! That's more than the population of most towns these days."

Crickets. The comedian had bombed before, walked away hungry on several occasions. He wasn't the funniest guy in the world, but usually, he could pull off something. He scanned the audience, his brain freezing until his eyes slid across the woman in the audience, the one who had been making eyes at him before. She wasn't bad looking for a waster, needed a shower or ten, but he decided to focus on her. Let the audience drift away, so it was only him and her.

He leaned into the microphone, letting his voice resonate, deep and rich. "Jobs. I don't even like the word. The worst thing about the word? Blowjobs."

"Yar!" a man in the audience yelled. You could always count on that guy, the pervert, the one who chuckled at the mere mention of anything dirty. It was a cheap trick, but the comedian wasn't too proud to go down that rabbit hole.

"Now, I don't know what genius was sitting around, talking to his buddies when he labeled this particular sex act, but if I had a time machine, and it only had one use, I would go back in time and slap the words right out of this guy's mouth before he could even utter them. Calling it a job makes it seem like work. No one wants to do work in bed. Sex is for after work, for most of us."

He had them leaning now. They listened, their eyes wide.

"Even worse, it spread like wildfire. First blowjobs, then hand jobs, foot jobs, armpit jobs, titty jobs. Next thing you know, every sexual act is an onerous task of debasement that has to be performed out of duty. That's no way to go about it. No way at all. Am I right?"

The people in the audience nodded.

"Man, if I had a time machine, I'd hop right in that fucker, press a few buttons, get that thing up to 88.8 miles-per-hour and—ZOOM!—I'm hitting up the 1960s, poppin' into some scene like out of an old movie. Buncha assholes are standing around preening over their muscle cars, Chubby Checker's playin' on the radio, and they're all sitting around talking about what base they got to with Peggy Sue."

The comedian was going now, flowing, weaving his spell as he spoke. His body wandered the stage, the largest he'd ever performed on, and he was getting every inch out of it, strutting and talking, all the time, keeping his eyes

55

locked on the woman with the large muddy eyes. He didn't need to make anyone else laugh, just her.

"And that's another thing. The base system. Who the fuck came up with this thing? Like no one knows what the bases are, right? I mean first base. That's kissing right? I think we all know first base, but then right after that, it all goes to shit. Second base. What the fuck is that? Hand under the shirt, hand over the shirt, hand down the pants? Hand up the pants? Hand in pocket? We don't fucking know. If there's going to be a system, there should have been a poster presented to us when we were kids. This shit should have been covered in sex ed when we were all eleven or twelve. This was the important shit. I don't need to know about vas deferens and ovaries. Tell me the about the fucking base system."

"Instead, I've got Holly Homeschool asking, 'Why do they call them nuts?' The teacher stammers, tries to keep from laughing, meanwhile, there's an entire sweet system of sexual levels goin' unaddressed, while the unlucky, cursed bastard forced to teach sex ed is stammering and hemming and hawing. God, now that's gotta be the worse job ever, right? Teaching sex ed? There's not a lot of people who are glad the world's dead, but I bet these sex ed teachers are. They're sitting in a bombed-out Pizza Hut, munchin' on a can of Alpo they found in a shed, and they're all, 'Phew! Glad that's over with.'"

A small titter from the crowd.

"So second base. We know it's something under the clothes, right? We can guess at that. It seems pretty obvious, but then you get to third base, and everything goes to shit. What the fuck is third? Hands, mouths, a little dry rub until completion. Pictures? A nice boudoir spread fit to be printed in *Spread It* magazine? Fully disrobing? Fingers in places? Not sayin' where. That's your business. What is it? I mean, if we're going to do this base system right, we're going to need like ten more bases. What base is spanking?

It certainly comes after kissing, right? Maybe. I don't know how you do it. I'm not in your bedroom. But you can spank someone with clothes on, right? So maybe there should just be a little base between first and second called first-and-a-half base. You're sittin' around, locker room talkin' with your buddies because you're a little dick man who never thought you were gonna get laid in the first place, so you're braggin' about it. You're letting everyone know you're a viable member of society, even though you're not. You're givin' everybody the juicy details, but you're unimaginative and basic, so you say, 'And then'—the comedian leans into his microphone—'I got to first-and-a-half base.'

"Wild applause go up from your friends, also a bunch of neanderthal, Cro-Magnon worms, and everyone agrees that yes, you are a part of society. It feels good… until one of your buddies stands up and says, 'Yeah, first-and-a-half is good, but check this.'" The comedian looks around conspiratorially. "'I just got to third!'"

The comedian's eyes went wide and his head shook with shock. "What the fuck is third? No one knows. It could be anything." The comedian found his girl in the audience. "You there. Miss. What do you think third base is?"

The woman, put on the spot, looked around, frantic and wide-eyed. Finally, a random word spilled out of her mouth. "Plungers?"

The comedian, unprepared for such a response, let his mouth drop open. "Plungers?" Shock and amusement dripped out of him, and he didn't hold it back. "Careful with this one, fellas, am I right? Plungers. Ok… third base is plungers. You got kissing at first, under the clothes at second, spanking at first-and-a-half… and then plungers, whatever the fuck that is."

"Of course, this brings up a whole new problem. Like… plungers for me as a man, is probably a whole lot different than plungers for a woman, am I right?"

To his right, off the edge of the stage, he heard Yokel say, "Maybe."

Trying not to get distracted, he forged ahead. "Let's be honest, the reason the base system isn't completely understood is because it's archaic. No one's played baseball since the vampiric rift opened up in Yellowstone." He paused, letting the laughter roll over him. That Yellowstone line got 'em every time. One of his heavy-hitters so to say. "One-size does not fit all. Like a base-system for me isn't going to be the same as for a woman, right? What's a home run for a dude?"

The comedian held the microphone out to the audience. Many different responses were yelled out, from the obligatory "Fucking!" to one wasteland-accented fellow screaming the word "Rogering." The word caught the comedian by surprise, and he mouthed it to the crowd. "Rogering. Jesus. That's a weird way to say fucking. Hey, baby, wanna come over and Roger tonight? That doesn't sound right, does it? You drop the I-N-G off rogering and it changes the whole thing. Lemme try this again."

In his best wasteland accent, that comedic patois of Michael Caine crossed with a bubble-town, sour whore, the comedian spoke into his microphone. "Ere now, wanna come over to me newspaper stuffed mattress and have a good rogering?"

The comedian shook with mock chills. "Nope. No rogering. That's awful. I implore each and every one of you to never use the word rogering for sex. It's wrong, all fucking wrong."

"So we all agree, a home run for a man, a straight man, is straight sex, straight pounding in the bits. But what if I was to ask you what a home run was for a woman?"

"Rogering!" one particularly dim looking man yelled.

"Maybe for you, pal, but not for *your* partner, and when I say not for *your* partner, I really mean it. I don't

58

think anyone would consider what you have to offer a home run. More of a bunt really." The comedian laughed as he held up his pinky finger.

Offended, the waster yelled out, "I gives it good!"

The comedian laughed as he held up his pinky finger. "I can see it comin' out the side of your loin cloth pal. Looks like you're rollin' with a pink Hot Tamale down there.

The crowd exploded at this, pointing and laughing at the poor guy.

The comedian moved on. "So what is it ladies? What's a home run?"

The muddy-eyed woman yelled, "Climax!"

"There it is folks. A climax, a toe-curling, body-convulsing climax. Now, that's a little different for a man, right. If a dude has a short fuse, there's a chance he might get a 'home run' on first-base, second-base, most definitely on third. But for women, they need a whole new base-system. After first, that damn thing splits off depending on your gender. Kissing, yeah, yeah. That's first. But what the hell is second base for women? And that's what's wrong with all the sexual terms we have these days. They were all invented by men."

"So I tell you what I'm going to do. I'm going to travel back in time and reinvent the sexual wheel. Come with me."

The comedian walked over to an imaginary DeLorean, lifted the door. He mimed starting the car and pressed a bunch of imaginary buttons, all accompanied by beeps and boops. He floored the invisible accelerator, zooming engine noises escaping his lips. "Whoosh!"

Hopping out of his imaginary car as if on a mission, the comedian strolled across the stage. "Hey there," he said to an imaginary man. "I hear you all are talking about sex."

Quickly, the comedian flipped around, playing the role of one of the imaginary men. "What's it to you, chum?" he said in an overly deep voice.

"Well, I'm here to stop you from ruining sex for everyone in the future."

Flip.

"Because I'm so good?"

Flip.

"No. Because you're an idiot. What you are about to say will have repercussions for every English-speaking person from now until the end of the world, which is in about 70 years, give or take."

Flip.

"Oh, come on. I don't see how one blow—"

Flip.

"Stop right there, my white-bread, thoughtless amigo. Instead of saying what you were just about to say, why don't you call it a gift?"

Flip.

"A gift?"

Flip.

"Yes, a gift. Because, if you call it a job, then you've taken something wonderful, and slippery and wet and warm, and you've turned into an act of debasement, something embarrassing and degrading. But if you call it a gift, well, then it's treasure, an act of love, a sign of devotion."

Flip.

"Fuck that. I want to debase and degrade."

Flip.

"Oh, really."

Flip.

"Yeah."

Flip.

"Ok." The comedian pulled an invisible shotgun from out of the air, made a cocking noise, and aimed it at his imaginary counterpart. "Well, how 'bout a gun job, buddy?" The comedian fired.

Flip.

The comedian, now playing the jock of the past, flew through the air and landed on his back with a thump. With his dying last words, he said, "I guess I could call it a gift." After performing a comical death, with much gasping and full-on legs kicking in the air, he lay still on the stage.

The crowd applauded, and the comedian hopped to his feet, taking a deep bow. "So when you're out there, getting' it on with whoever or whatever, and you're doing your business, maybe breaking out the plungers, remember, it's a gift! It should be something given. And the next time you hear one of these troglodytes call something a job, tell 'em it's only a job because no one actually wants to fuck 'em."

With the audience warmed up, they showered him with a healthy dose of applause. Meanwhile, he sensed a surge of energy throughout the audience. Whether they knew it or not, every single person in the audience was now horny, now thinking of sex, of gifts given, and bases rounded. Everything he said afterward would be forgotten, remembered as it was spoken and then vanished into the ether as their minds turned back to sex. It was the curse of the dirty comedian, to get people riled up and then have them forget the rest of your set as the blood from their brains settled into their naughty bits. But fuck, when you were dying on stage, you had to do something.

From there, he went into his bits about raiders, about Chicken Kickers, about all the tough-ass names everyone came up with. Although, everyone in Ike seemed to have some sort of Scandinavian name, so the bit fell a little flat when he couldn't find someone named Razorburn or Machete.

Over the course of the evening, the comedian wove his spell, moving about, dancing and waving his hands like a magician executing a spell. The audience ate it up, while the woman with the muddy eyes tracked his movements across the stage. He had a fan.

Then, for the coup de grace, the comedian had Yokel lug his tiny, pathetic piano onto the stage. The comedian sat next to it, legs crossed, like Schroeder on the Peanuts cartoons, and he plucked out a tune to end the night.

> Meatly-meatly-meat.
> I'm losin' all my meat.
> Meatly-meatly-meat.
> I'm losin' all my meat.
> Meatly-meatly-meat.
> I'm losin' all my meat.
> Meatly-meatly-meat.
> I'm losin' all my meat.
> He rots on the blacktop all day long,
> Rottin' and a boppin' and a singing his song.
> All the other lepers on Leper Street,
> Love to see ol' Robin lose his meat.
> Rotten Robin. Meat, meat, meat.
> Rotten Robin. Meatly, meatly, meat.
> I'm losin' all my meat.
> 'Cause we're really gonna rot tonight!
> Every little pinkie, every little toe
> Every piece of skin and even his nose
> The wise old leper, the ancient crone
> Flappin' their gums singin', "Go Rob go."
> Rotten Robin. Meat, meat, meat.
> Rotten Robin. Meatly, meatly, meat.
> I'm losin' all my meat.
> 'Cause we're really gonna rot tonight!
> A pretty little raider picked up his hand
> Taught him how to eat it, and it was grand
> He started chompin' on it, and bless my soul
> He spit the knuckles out into a bowl.

He rots on the blacktop all day long
Rottin' and a-boppin' and a-singing his song
All the other lepers on Leper Street
Love to see Robin lose his meat.
Rotten Robin. Meat, meat, meat.
Rotten Robin. Meatly, meatly, meat.
I'm losin' all my meat.
'Cause we're really gonna rot tonight!

As the comedian finished and the last echoes of his voice and the Fetus Grand faded into the upper reaches of Ike's rafters, a silence fell over the entire town. And then it came, an ocean of applause, washing over him, and behind his goggles, the beginnings of small tears gathered at the corners of his eyes.

He stood, bowing like the conductor of a great symphony, and who was to say that his music, his song, was not the greatest performed that day? When he bowed, he peeked into the audience, appreciating the five people who applauded. The rest of the wasters were already stalking down the Long Natural Path, disappearing from whence they'd come.

"Before you go, if you enjoyed the show, please leave a donation!" But most of the people ignored him, drifting back into the rest of the store like the baseball players at the end of *Field of Dreams*, vanishing among piles of furniture and bookcases and knickknacks. The comedian turned and began tearing down his lights.

"Start rounding up all the shit they threw," he whispered to Yokel. Immediately, Yokel began scampering around the stage picking up hex bolts and Allen wrenches. "And don't forget my pomato."

As he worked, Kallax appeared at his elbow. "It was a good thing you did today."

"Didn't do it to be good."

"I know, but it was good anyway. The customers can sometimes be restless."

63

"Customers?"

"Oh, yeah. Store's full of 'em. The ones without shirts."

These people are weird, Oddrey whispered.

The comedian finished spooling up his lights and pulled them over his head so they would hang around his torso. He bent down and picked up his Fetus Grand. "Well, the show is done. Didn't get much out of it, and if we're to go on this"—he hesitated to say the word, it revolted him so much—"quest, we're going to need some fuel. You know what I mean?"

The robed man nodded. "I know precisely." Kallax clapped his hands, and a couple of "customers" appeared with bowls of something soft and swirly in their dirty hands. The comedian took his without saying a word, while Ajax and Yokel grabbed theirs and offered a small thanks.

A spoon stuck out of the pinkish pile of goo. The comedian grabbed the spoon and played with the ooze a little bit. Watching the goop drip from the tip of the spoon, he asked, "What is it?"

"Protein fuel. We make it here. We all eat it."

"Show me."

Kallax reached out for the spoon in the comedian's hand, and he snatched it away. "Not with my spoon, weirdo."

The robed man shrugged and reached into one of the folds sewn into his old carpet robe, producing a spoon. He reached out, dipped it in the faintly red goo, and then placed it in his mouth. "Mmmm, mmmm, pure protein," he managed to say after he choked it down.

"And you all eat this?" the comedian asked dubiously.

"Look around. Not a lot of options out here."

The comedian nodded, then sighed, looking at the pile of pink shit. "It's people, isn't it?"

Kallax shrugged, tapped the side of his nose and gave him a wink.

"It's good!" a delighted Yokel announced. Yokel sat on the edge of the stage, his feet kicking in the air, his head bobbing from side to side as he ate. Ajax, somewhat doubtful, kept dipping her spoon in the goop, holding it in the air, and letting the slop fall back into the bowl with a splat.

"Well, thank you for the food." The comedian hopped off the stage and took a seat next to Yokel, despite the revolting slurping sounds as the man ate. Kallax sat next to the comedian, executing a perfect old man groan. Their business wasn't done yet.

"Now you wanna tell me about this"—the comedian held back his gorge—"quest?"

"Man who took the treasure was a yellow shirt. One of the best. Name's Klampenborg. He's a sly sort. We got an inkling he fled to our competitor in Alma."

"Alma? Where's that?"

Kallax's eyes rolled back in his head as he tried to access the information in his withered brain. "Oh, it's, uh, let's say about ten miles due north, south."

"North south?"

"Yeah, directions are weird out here. I swear the sun comes up in a different place every day. Like we're on a merry-go-round."

He's got canni-brain, Oddrey said.

"You have a guide who could lead us there?" the comedian asked. "I mean ten miles north south doesn't mean much to me."

"I have just the person." Kallax clapped his hands, and just as he expected, the woman with the muddy eyes appeared. Her face was oval-shaped, her cheekbones jutting out, making her face long and horse-ish. Her hair hung in greasy black tangles, framing her face. Black circles ringed

65

her eyes, and over all of this, a layer of grime dimmed her olive skin.

"This is Vagsjon."

"Do what now?"

"Vaj-is-jon. It's from the catalogue."

At the confusion around her name, Vagsjon stood with her head down, her hair blocking her face, though the comedian thought he caught a slight flushing underneath all the grit and grime. "The catalogue. Right."

"What in Sam Heck is the catalogue?" Yokel asked.

Kallax nodded good-naturedly. For a cannibal, he was quite the nice guy. "It's the holy book. All of our children are named after the names in the book. Some of the names can be confusing, and the correct way of speaking them has been lost, but we do the best we can."

"Alright, lemme see if I got everything figured out," the comedian began. "You want me to take Vagine…"

"Vagsjon," Kallax corrected.

"…to someplace called Alma, where I am to find a dude named Klampenborg, retrieve a brick of silver, and then come on back. Hopefully, by then, Cheatums will be done with this natural path business…"

"The *Long* Natural Path," Kallax interjected.

"What do you want me to do with Klampenborg when I see him? Her? They?"

"Quitters must be punished, yes? He didn't even give his two weeks," Kallax scoffed.

"Of course," the comedian mocked. "It all makes perfect sense."

Kallax nodded in agreement. "Enjoy your protein fuel and get some rest. The road between Ike and Alma… is not always easy. No one will disturb you. Rest well, and good luck on your quest."

"Thanks, Mister," Yokel said around another spoonful of protein fuel. Kallax nodded, waved a gnarled

66

hand at them and then shambled down the Long Natural Path.

"I thought he'd never leave," the comedian said.

Maybe he hasn't, Oddrey said.

The comedian knew exactly what Oddrey was getting at. Vagine, or whatever the hell her name was, was most likely a spy for Kallax and whatever weird cult they had going on in Ike.

"Here," the comedian said. "You can have my soylent pink." The comedian passed his protein fuel to Yokel who was licking his own bowl clean. The cinematist snatched it up and went to town like a hungry dog with a fresh bone.

It's made of people! Oddrey cackled in his mind.

Ajax, done picking up protein fuel and plopping it into her bowl with her spoon, set hers down on the stage while the comedian studied Vagine.

She stood with her head down, looking like a Japanese movie ghost, and already the comedian felt annoyed by her. Meekness. He hated it, found it to be the most disgusting of human traits, besides a lack of a sense of humor.

"What do you have to say?" the comedian asked.

"It is my pleasure to guide you."

"Well, I suppose you'll want to be sleeping with me."

At this, Vagine raised her head, her eyes large and fearful. "Oh, no."

The comedian, taken aback by her response, tried to recover. "But I uh, I saw the way you were looking at me. I mean, people have looked at me like that before, and, uh, I was just joking. Like a whole bunch. Forget I said anything."

Vagine, seeing the comedian stammer and make a fool of himself, tried to downplay the comedian's mistake. "Oh, is not cuz I don't have like fer ya. I mean, I does.

67

You's not dirty and tings. But, it's just, my heart goes to another."

"It's not me, is it?" Yokel asked, a hint of fear coming into his voice.

"Shut up, guy. No one's into you like that," the comedian said.

"Someone could be," Yokel said.

"I believe the comedian is correct," Ajax added.

Yokel took in the knowledge, looked sad for a second, and then went back at the protein fuel, slurping up the drippy, goopy mess, his feet kicking back and forth as they dangled off the stage.

"Well. I'm glad your heart belongs to someone else. We've got a job to do after all, can't have romance getting in the way of some good old-fashioned questing, now can we?"

You thought she wanted you, Oddrey giggled.

"Shut up, Odd," the comedian whispered out the corner of his mouth, as Vagine cocked her head.

"Who is Odd?"

"You're fucking odd," the comedian spat at Vagine.

"Oh, then I shut up."

Exhaustion overcame the comedian then, sudden and keen. He let a deep sigh escape from his chest, as the veneer of the showman melted away, leaving behind the Broken Man. His pain, gone for a few hours, hurtled back into him like a meteorite smacking into the earth, and the ever-present smile fell from his face. Without a word to the others, he grabbed his gear and headed to a place behind the stage, as far from the Long Natural Path as he could find. There, he made his bed.

****

Ajax saw the change overcome the comedian and knew his brokenness had caught up to him.

"Come." she said. "We should all rest. We have a long way to go tomorrow."

The Ikean nodded her head as did Yokel, who burped, patted his belly, and then lay down on the stage. Ajax made her bed some distance from all of them as she relived the embarrassment of the show. She had wondered why the comedian didn't teach her how to juggle, though he knew the ways of it, and now she had her answer. He had thrown her to the proverbial rad stags without so much as a word of encouragement, and she struggled to contain her fury. Though it had all turned out well, and she had even received a smattering of applause, she didn't like to be used.

Should I talk to him about it? Or should I let it go? The comedian's ways were wrong, cruel, emotionless. If she was ever to mend that which was broken, she might need to fix this. Emotion was the heat that melted the steel of the soul. A broken soul could not be mended without the heat of emotion. But was he ready for it? Or would he retreat, disappear, go deeper into the void of his own brain if she challenged him?

Ajax didn't know the answers, and as she pondered the questions, she rolled over on her back and peered into the dim light of the rafters. It was dark outside now, and the rafters were mostly cloaked in shadows, but above, she could sense the rafter people looking down at her.

A strange place, this Ike. But all places are strange outside The Coop.

She yearned for home at that moment, her heart clenching with longing for the green fields, the *cluck cluck* of chickens, and the comforting sounds of steel striking steel as the youths trained for their turn in the wild. She wondered if her friends Comet and Silver had made it back to The Coop.

Have they talked to Mother, told her I went my own way? Does she still love me in her own hard manner?

69

These questions caused her more pain than comfort, and she closed her eyes to hide the specter of people hanging in the sky. Time enough for questions. Tomorrow, we see Alma, whatever that is.

****

In the corner of the courtyard, Vagsjon cried. There were many reasons for the poor girl to cry, the first of which was her own twisting, battered heart. In its depths, the pain of the impossible burned, and though she pined for the unattainable, knew it could never happen, a glimmer of hope dwelled in her chest, fanning the flames of her pain.

She had been chosen for a specific reason by the yellow shirts, who took their commands from the regional manager. That reason had caused her no end of grief, and now she was being thrown to the cats because she had nothing to offer the cashiers, nothing with which to pay for her continued existence.

This too caused her sadness, but mostly, it was the first thing. Vagsjon didn't have a word for that thing, didn't know how to name the feeling in her chest. It was almost like the "duty" the yellow shirts spoke of—almost, but not quite—a feeling of desire and responsibility. Mixed in was something else though, a thought of the future, of how the world could be perfect if only the object of her desire would desire her in kind. *Oh, there gots to be a word for it.*

She went through the limited vocabulary in her mind, but none of the words she knew could quite encapsulate the depth or meaning of her emotions.

Eventually, she stuffed her feelings down and found a new hope smoldering there. *I'm going home.*

****

Yokel rolled on the stage, his guts churning. Today had been a good day, perhaps too good. All he wanted to do was bask in the glory of his performance, of the acceptance, but the pain was too great.

In the dim of Ike, his pain on display on the stage for all to see, he heard a voice. Small and soothing, he listened to it as it spoke to him, let the voice's syllables wash over him like a spell. His stomach stopped rumbling, the cramps fading away to nothing more than slight discomfort. Eventually, he fell into a restful dream, the smell of popcorn washing over him, the sound of kernels popping in the dim of a movie theater, the rickety run of a projector rolling on into the night.

Chapter 4: Road to Alma

The comedian awoke with the first ray of sunlight shining through the dirty glass doors of Ike. He hated the morning sun, always felt it was a little sharper than at any other point in the day. Walking in morning sun actually seemed to sting. Maybe even the sun was trying to kill them, although, he guessed that had been a truth for a while. Everything was deadly these days, even himself, although as he sat up, groaning and tight from sleeping on a concrete floor all night, he didn't feel particularly lethal. The road would loosen him up though.

"Rise and shine," he called to the others, hating himself a little bit.

Ajax snapped to, hopped to her feet, and began preparing for the journey. On the stage, Yokel sat up with a groan, rubbing at his head.

"I don't feel so good."

The comedian ignored the man, as he didn't actually care how he felt. As far as he was concerned, Yokel's part in his life was over.

Vagine sat up, looking even filthier in the daylight somehow. She rubbed at the dark circles under her eyes and stood on two filthy feet, the toenails gnarled and jagged. He hoped that whatever wind there was today, hopefully not the misty, "drown in your own memories" kind, he would be upwind of her.

The funk of Ike lay heavy that morning as the waste sun warmed up the building. Above, people hung from the rafters, secured in strange harnesses, sleeping like vampire bats. He pondered the ridiculousness of Ike, a former home furnishings store turned into some sort of strange tribal culture. The people here had picked up the corporate oddities of a mega corporation and now clung to them like a granny on her deathbed seeking the last rites before she passed on. It was sad really, how people needed these things—a role, a place in society and rules to follow. Oh, you could try and change their minds, but even though the ideas of freedom had been lauded for centuries, when it came down to it, your average human needed to be told what to do, needed someone in control. Or else they turned into weapon-toting madmen and women. That's what raiders were, the people who loved freedom so much, they were willing to jab it in your ribs and twist. One person's freedom was another person's suffering.

"You ready to go, T.C.?" Yokel asked.

"Gimme a sec," the comedian said. "And don't call me T.C."

"You got it, T.C."

The comedian held back a scream of frustration. It wouldn't do any good now, and he needed to limber up before he stepped back into the blasted landscape of the waste, with its dry hills, strange plant and animal life, and danger around every corner. A good stretch was just the thing to get the blood flowing.

As he moved about, flexing the muscles in his legs, back and shoulders, he came alive, the memory of last night flooding his mind. He smiled as he stretched his quads, thinking about the way Ajax had dodged the bolts and wrenches thrown in her direction. *Dodge, Duck, Dip, Dive, and Dodge.*

As he placed one arm across his body and pulled on it to loosen up his shoulders, he made eye contact with her. Her head cocked to the side, and he realized he was smiling at her. Quickly he wiped the smile from his face.

Bending over and stretching his hamstrings to their fullest, he rankled at the idea of another quest. *A fucking quest. Every goddamn time. Just once I'd like to stroll into a town, and not have to do some bastard's menial labor. Just give me what I want for once.*

Would you really like that? Oddrey asked.

73

"Of course."

No you wouldn't. You'd find some way to be pissed off about it. It's your natural state.

"Whatever."

Can you finish this stretch now? All the blood is rushing into my head."

"Ha ha. Good one, Odd. Where else would your blood be?

I hate you.

The comedian finished his stretching, wondering if what Oddrey said was true. Was he incapable of being happy? He didn't think so, but he didn't have any proof to the contrary either.

As he shouldered his gear, Vagine strolled up behind him. He knew she was there before she even spoke, thanks to the stench. "Who were you talking to?"

"Oh, uh, nobody."

"You were talking to that doll head, weren't you?"

"Let's not get personal here. We got a job to do, and we're gonna do it. Let's leave it at that."

Vagine shrugged, and the comedian clapped his hands, a puff of waste dust clouding from his palms. "Well, shall we hit it?"

"Hit what?" Ajax asked.

"I don't want to be hit," Vagine said.

"No... God." The comedian put a fingerless-gloved hand to his forehead, already dreading the day. "*Hit it* means get out on the road. It's a saying."

"It's not one that I've ever heard of," Ajax said.

"Me neither," Vagine added.

"That's because neither of you hangs out with anyone cool like me. I say all sorts of cool shit. Try soaking some of it up, and maybe you too can be cool one day. So? Shall we hit it?"

Vagine nodded, her creepy eyes as round as two moons. Ajax shrugged her shoulders and began plodding in the direction of the doors. Yokel followed along.

"Whoa, whoa, whoa. Where the hell do you think you're going?"

Confused, Yokel said, "I'm gonna hit it, T.C."

"The hell you are. You're staying right here."

"But you'll need me."

"We don't even know what we're walking into out there, and I can't... do my thing if I keep having to save people's asses, you know what I mean?"

"Well, what about Vagsjon—"

"Who?" the comedian asked.

Yokel pointed at Vagine.

"Oh, Vagine? Yeah, I don't care what happens to her."

A small smile broke on Yokel's face. "But you care what happens to me?"

The comedian saw no need to shatter the illusion, so he said, "Yeah, sure." The beaming of Yokel's face did something to the comedian, something he wasn't all that comfortable with. Somewhere in his cold, scarred heart, a tender green bud of friendship sprouted. "Besides, I need someone here in case they double-cross us. You've been here for how long?"

"A week."

"And they haven't killed you yet. If they try and lock us out, I'd rather have someone on the inside here. Especially if we have to run from another purrthquake."

He wasn't happy about it, but Yokel nodded his head. The comedian slapped him on the shoulder, hard enough to rock him on his feet.

With that, he turned, set the destination in his mind, and waved the others on. A couple of yellow shirts slid the glass doors open, and they stepped out into the waste, the smell of burnt civilization assaulting their noses, the sun beating down on them with fists made of ultraviolet rays. A harsh wind kicked up, sending the comedian's military jacket fluttering in the wind as abrasive grit scraped the sleep from his eyes.

"Which way?" he asked the girl.

She pointed in a direction, and they set out for Alma.

****

The walk was not a difficult one. A snaking path, well-trodden and devoid of plant-life, led through a valley of rocky hills dotted with stunted cactuses, needles as sharp as anything on the planet. The comedian didn't like it, thought it might be worth it to leave the easy path, climb to the top of the ridges and have a little more visibility.

But this was the path Vagine led them on, and it was quick. They moved at a good clip, and the valley protected them from the harsh sun, so that was a bonus. In the shade of the valley, it was cool, and he was thankful for his jacket for the thousandth time. He moved light without the weight of the Fetus Grand on his back. He'd left it back in Ike, trusting that Yokel would keep an eye on it.

You probably should have told him to guard it, Odd said.

"Maybe you're right. All the more reason to get this over and done with."

Vagine, who had been stumbling along ahead of them, turned and said, "You did it again."

"Did what?" the comedian griped.

"Talked to that doll head."

"It talks to him," Ajax said.

"I didn't hear anything."

"Only he can hear it."

Annoyed, the comedian, snapped, "Shut up, everyone."

76

"Is it a God?" Vagine asked.

The comedian, taken back by her question, did what he always did when he was uncomfortable. He ignored the question completely.

"I've heard peeps talkin' bout dese tings. Gods. Them says Gods talk to peeps, but only to certain people, people who be a-special."

"You're special."

"Thank you," Vagine said, her hand going to her heart in sincere gratitude.

Her simplicity annoyed the comedian. It seemed everyone in this world was getting stupider by the day. Vagine was just further proof of things going to shit, especially humanity.

"I don't think he meant it as a compliment," Ajax responded.

The smile fell from Vagine's face, and she looked genuinely hurt.

"Why'd you have to go and say that?" the comedian asked Ajax, miffed. Ahead, Vagine turned and focused on picking her way through the rocks on the ground. More than once, she had stepped on a particularly sharp rock with her bare feet, wincing and hopping in pain. The waste was not a place for the shoeless.

"What?" Ajax asked, confused by the comedian's response.

"You hurt her," the comedian said.

"What do you care?" Ajax retorted, acid in her words.

"Well, I don't."

"You insulted her. She misunderstood. I thought I was helping."

"Well, you didn't. And I don't need anyone explaining my words."

Ajax ignored him for the most part, and this annoyed him to no end. "You see, when I insult someone, it's funny. The insult is for me. Not them. If they don't get it, then that's good enough. You don't need to go around explaining it. That takes all the fun out of it."

"Fun?" Ajax asked. "It's fun to hurt people?"

The comedian sighed in frustration. "You know what? Yeah, it's fun to hurt people."

"Is that why you sent me up there to embarrass myself?"

The comedian threw his hands in the air as if giving up. "Oh, boy. Here we go. Give it to me. Say what you gotta say."

Ajax fell silent, chewing on the inside of her lip.

"Now you're quiet. Ha!"

After their exchange, they trudged on in silence, carving through the winding valley, each member of the group stuck in their own head. *Being around people is hard.* Suddenly, the comedian wanted nothing more than to turn around, run into Ike and slay everyone with Side-Splitter. It would be easier. If he was alone, it's what he would have done as soon as the regional manager told him he couldn't see Cheatums. Hell, he could do it right now. *Fuck these people. Fuck 'em all.*

You're scared, Oddrey accused.

The comedian refused to talk to Oddrey.

You're not talking to me because you don't want them to think you're crazy. Because you care what they think. Maybe you should start showing it before you drive them away.

He didn't disagree with Oddrey, but he didn't like what she said either.

"I'm sorry about the wrenches," he finally spat out.

The look of surprise on Ajax's face was almost worth it. Almost. "I just, I didn't want you to be nervous up there, and if I told you what I was planning, I knew you wouldn't even go through with it."

"You used me," Ajax said.

78

"Oh, now come on. Don't say it like that."

Ajax clammed up, and for the first time in decades, the comedian felt something he hadn't felt before, another emotion he had locked away. Shame. That's what happened when you started mixing with other people, tying your lives together, you got to experience a whole new set of emotions a lone wolf never experienced. Shame was one of those. Without other people, people you actually cared about—

Aw, you care about her, Oddrey cooed.

"Shut up," he spat.

Ajax cocked an eyebrow at him, and he said, "Yes, I used you."

"But it was for the best," Ajax continued, seemingly reading his mind.

"It was. And I... I apologize."

"Where I come from, apologies are not enough. When one does something wrong, we demand an act of atonement, an act of justice."

"Well, where I come from, we just say 'apology accepted' and pretend like everything is alright."

"Apology not accepted."

The comedian stopped in his tracks, shaking with frustration. *Why is this so hard?* Vagine and Ajax moved forward, leaving the comedian standing on his own. *An act of atonement. What the hell does that even mean?*

Maybe you could teach her how to actually juggle, Oddrey chimed in.

"Yeah, I could do that. I could also teach you gymnastics while I'm at it."

I'm flipping you off right now. You can't see it, but I definitely am.

Just then, he caught a flash of movement and a skittering out of the corner of his eye. When he turned, he saw it was just a tumbleweed rolling down the side of the valley. He would have ignored it completely if a gust of wind hadn't kicked up just then, sending dry dust floating through the air. But, despite this perfectly adequate gust of wind, the tumbleweed didn't change course. Even though a cloud of dust blew through its branchy body, it continued rolling straight at them. Then, on the valley's ridge, he caught sight of more shapes, rolling and tumbling against the wind.

He didn't wait after that, he took off running, his legs pumping up and down. The sound of the tumbleweeds rolling across the ground sounded faintly like chewing, a thousand hungry teeth eating up the earth.

"We got company!" the comedian yelled as he ran past Ajax and Vagine, or whatever the hell her name was. Soon, the trio was running pell-mell along the path at the bottom of the valley.

The tumbleweeds, despite the complete lack of arms or legs the comedian could see, managed to keep up with them. Ahead, the path curved, winding around a rocky spur. He kept his eyes locked on it, and then, to his right, he heard Vagine scream. When he turned toward her, she held her foot in her hand, a stone jutting up through the top of her foot and blood splattering on the ground where the thirsty earth swallowed it up.

"Shit." The comedian's first thought was to leave her in the dust, let the tumbleweeds have her. Against his better judgment, he ignored the voice and picked the sweaty, greasy woman off the ground, though he had to fight his gag reflex at the stench of her.

"You need a bath," the comedian said.

Oddrey corrected him. *She needs a firehose.*

Ajax ducked under Vagine's other shoulder, and they ran on, plowing across the path. The comedian only needed one look over his shoulder to know it was hopeless. Behind them, dozens of the tumbleweeds came on, rolling with a purpose no tumbleweed had ever had before.

The survivors managed to keep up their run for another couple hundred yards.

"Pick a spot," the comedian called.

Ajax pointed at a section of the valley wall where a natural break in the rocky walls formed a protective alcove. It would give them a place to make their stand. An overhead ledge would offer protection from attacks from above.

"Go! Go! Go!" he shouted. When they reached the shade of the overhang, they dumped Vagine to the ground. The comedian unsheathed Side-Splitter and stood at the ready, while Ajax did the same with her mace.

"The Holiest of Holys," he grumbled as the first of the tumbleweeds rolled within reach. He swung his blade, as large as an airplane propeller and just as deadly. The metal crashed into the rolling ball, shattering a couple of branches and sending it sailing into the air. But more came. Out of the corner of his eye, he saw Ajax swing downward, smashing a tumbleweed with a loud, branchy crunch. It contracted, then popped right back into its normal shape like a spring, rolling away drunkenly, as if it had a concussion.

From there, all went blank as the two warriors swung and smashed, bashed and chopped, holding a never-ending tide of carnivorous weeds at bay. It was a losing battle, but the comedian didn't care. He would go down swinging.

"I always knew I was gonna die one day. Just didn't think it would be at the hands of a bunch of murderous tumbleweeds."

Ajax flattened another of the weeds, but didn't respond.

"You got any clever names for these things, Odd?" The comedian let loose a mammoth roar, and pebbles and dust sifted down from the rocky overhang above.

Nope.

After a while, the weeds, seeing they couldn't get anywhere on their own, regrouped at the opposite side of the valley floor. Then, wonder of wonders, they began bunching up, rolling on top of each other, their spindly little branches interlocking. The comedian, sensing an opening, let Side-Splitter drop to the ground.

"What are you doing?" Ajax gasped, her breathing heavy, sweat dripping off her arms. Vagine huddled in the back, bleeding from her foot and whimpering, her eyes squeezed shut.

"Only gonna get one chance at this." The comedian reached into his jacket pocket and pulled out a long cylindrical tube.

"What is that?"

"A Roman candle."

"Are you ok? Can you not see? It's plenty bright out. Maybe take your goggles off."

The comedian ignored her, dug around in his pocket for one of his few remaining treasures. His hands clasped upon a square shape. He pulled the pack of matches out, straightened the fuse of the roman candle, and as the last tumbleweed climbed aboard the rolling ball, he screamed a challenge at the tumbleweeds, now more like a tumbleboulder. "Come and get it!"

He pulled one of the cardboard matches free, placed it between thumb and forefinger, and dragged it along the striker stripe. Nothing happened. Pebbles and rocks crunched underneath the tumbleboulder as it rolled onward. Figuring he had a dud, the comedian let the match drop to the ground and pulled another from the book. He struck the new match to the same result.

"Well, shit," he managed to say as the tumbleboulder rammed into them with all the force of a rather large dog. It knocked them backward and off their feet, and then the tumbleboulder broke apart. All over their bodies, the tumbleweeds crawled, pricking and poking their flesh. In his head, the comedian thought he heard the faint sound of giggling, but he put this down to the fact he might actually be insane. Ajax and Vagine screamed, and he added his own voice to the chorus as one of the tumbleweeds scratched his cheek. "Not my face!"

Eventually, the tumbleweeds, lacking teeth or stomachs or any actual need to feed, rolled away when they became bored. The trio of survivors sat in the shade of the overhang, traumatized and confused. The comedian sat up, panicked. He brushed the bits of tumbleweed detritus off his jacket, pulled his goggles from his head and angled the lenses so he could see his face in the reflection of one of the goggle's lenses.

Ajax laughed at him then, the first laugh he had ever heard her utter.

"This is what you laugh at?" the comedian asked her, shocked and flabbergasted as he continued the study of his cheek.

"You are like one of those painted whores in the fleshtowns, worrying about your face."

"This is my money-maker. People like this face. Trust it. If it gets all messed up, I might as well be a raider." The comedian lightly touched a finger to his face, and Ajax giggled some more. "Do you think it's going to scar?"

Another giggle.

"You have the worst sense of humor of anyone who ever lived."

Ajax turned her back on him and his ministrations. She bent to pull Vagine to her feet. "Are you ok?" she asked.

The girl, looking nothing like someone who felt ok, nodded her head, her eyes large and freaky.

Eventually, the comedian judged that the wound wouldn't scar, so long as it didn't become infected and he avoided picking at it. He put his gogs back on and stood, dusting himself off once more. "Painted whores," he grumbled. "I get a scar on my face, everyone's going to think I'm a stupid raider, or some worthless waster like..." The comedian was about to insult Vagine, but then thought better of it when he saw her face.

Instead, he asked her if she knew of any more surprises.

"I don't know much 'bout the Open," she said. "Only been in the Open this many times." Vagine held up two fingers. "Yeller shirts maybe know. They come out sometimes."

"The open? You mean outside? You've only been outside twice?"

Vagine nodded her head. For the first time, the comedian felt something other than revulsion for Vagine. Now, he felt pity. "Do you know this town, this Alma?" the comedian asked.

The girl, her greasy body now covered in dust like she was trying to hide from the Predator, rubbed self-consciously at the scratches on her arms. She nodded meekly.

"What can you tell us about it?" Ajax asked.

"I'm not supposed to say."

"Says who?"

But the girl wouldn't speak. Ajax stalked over to her, gripped her by the upper arms and looked deep into her eyes. "Not telling is the same as lying. You know what I have to do to those who lie?"

"Jesus, Ajax," the comedian said, taken aback by her rough talk with the girl.

"I have to kick them. Kick them until they tell me what I want to know. Do you want to tell me, or do you want to get kicked?"

Vagine looked down at the boots on Ajax's feet. They were scuffed and worn, but they would hurt.

Tears brimmed in Vagine's eyes, and as quiet as a whisper, she said, "If I sayin', you promise not to rat me to the yeller shirts?"

"I promise," Ajax said immediately.

The comedian, not one for making promises, shrugged his shoulders.

"You have to promise," Vagine said.

"I don't have to do shit."

"Just promise," Ajax said, "or we'll be sitting here all night."

"No promises. It's against my nature."

"I've noticed," Ajax said. Then she turned back to the girl. "Listen, I promise for him and me. If he tries to tell, I'll stop him."

"You can try," the comedian muttered.

"Now what can you tell us about Alma?"

"Not much," the girl began, and the comedian shook his head and scoffed in annoyance. "I's from there before... 'fore I could 'member."

"What does that mean?" the comedian asked. He was having a hard time understanding the gibberish coming out of her mouth.

"I was...b-b-born there," Vagine whispered.

"How did you end up in Ike?" Ajax asked.

The comedian saw a glimmer of excitement in Ajax's eyes. "You're getting off on this, aren't you? Acting like some sort of big shit detective."

"We should know what we're walking into," Ajax said.

The comedian scoffed once more. All they were doing was wasting time. The comedian already knew what awaited him in Alma, another group of ragtag wasters with weird rules, some dipshit in charge, and probably another fucking quest waiting for them. Nothing this slip of a girl could tell them would make any difference.

85

"Ike goes to Alma, the yeller shirts, every few years. They go there, and they take the young ones."

"Why do they take them?" Ajax asked.

Why does anyone take another human being? The comedian already knew the answers. *Sex, labor, food.*

"They need 'em in Ike, need 'em to make the protein fuel to keep everyone alive."

"What's in the protein fuel?" Ajax asked.

"I mustn't say. The yeller shirts'll hurt me."

"It's babies isn't it?" the comedian asked.

He didn't need an answer to know he was correct, as Vagine's eyes grew even wider than he thought was possible. Any second now, her eyeballs were going to pop right out of her head and roll around on the dusty ground.

"But you can't make babies, so no protein fuel, so you're expendable, right?" the comedian asked.

Vagine put her hands to her head to block out the comedian's words.

"You die out here, they don't care. Just one less mouth to feed. When the pack starts getting thin or sickly, they just roll up to Alma and snatch a new batch, right?"

Vagine wrapped her arms around herself, nodded with her head down, tears spilling from her eyes.

Ajax glared at him, as if he might not be a human but something one might find on the bottom of their shoe after walking through a sewer.

"Now, one thing I do want to know is if you've seen Cheatums?"

"Cheatums?" Vagine asked.

"Lanky man, about yay tall, cocky son of a bitch. At first look, he seems handsome, then you look again, and you realize he might be the ugliest bastard you've ever met. At first, he's all charming, but he can't help himself. Turns into a real shitsack after a while. Your boss said he went down the Long Natural Path. Now what the hell is that?"

86

"Oh, no. I can't say you that," Vagine said. She scanned the valley around her, as if yellow shirts were sitting just over the ridgeline, listening to their conversation.

"But you've seen him?"

Vagine nodded her head. "I's peeped 'im, gamble man, the type of bruh who inserts the wrench wrong. I's peeped him and the other one."

"The other one?" the comedian asked.

"His bruh. Not like bruh, bruh, but actual bruh. The handsome man. The like of this one's life."

"Beatums? Beatums is here?"

The mousy girl's head bobbed up and down, her head drooping and strands of her greasy hair hiding her face once more. "Him took the path, goin' after his bruh."

The comedian sat back, digesting the news. Earlier, when the regional manager had said five people had shown up in town, he had put it down to the son of a bitch not being able to count. He was a manager after all, the lowest of the low, the type of guy who walked on the backs of his employees while they did all the work, living off their labors while pretending he was something more than just a dude who had lucked into a job.

Ajax bent on one knee, and with one hand, tilted Vagine's head up by the chin. "What *is* the Long Natural Path, Vagsjon?"

"What'd you just call her? Her name's Vagine."

The girl shook her head, breaking free of Ajax's grip. "Can't say."

"Why not?"

"A-cause there's another path, and if they knows I's sayin', they'll put me on it, and then they'll eat me. The Short Unnatural Path is not one you want to be on."

"We won't tell," Ajax cooed. "And there's no one out here to hear but us."

"I won't tell," the comedian assured her.

87

"You promise to save Beatums, my one and only true like?"

The comedian looked off into the distance, blew out his cheeks a bit, and tried to do anything but look at Vagine.

"You have to promise!" Vagine yelled.

The comedian mumbled something as he pretended to look at something off in the distance. "I don't do promises."

Ajax glared at him, and he shrugged his shoulders and spread his arms wide. "What? It's my thing. I don't tell you to stop walking around all serious and weird, do I?"

"They's gonna to turn him into meatballs!" Vagine wailed, her body sobbing with the revelation.

The comedian took one of his fingers and jabbed it in his ear, wiggling it around to break up the earwax that was clearly causing him to hear things incorrectly. "Say that again."

"The long natural path, it's really just a way to…"

"To what?" Ajax prodded.

"To make the meat taste better."

"And Cheatums and Beatums are both on this path?" Ajax asked.

"Cheatums, him come first. He's further along the path, six days or so. 'Nother day, and he'll be ready. Beatums, showed up the day before you did. Once he heared his bruh'd taken the path, he demanded to take it as well."

The comedian rubbed his hand across his face, lost in thought.

Ajax stood, forgetting the girl for a moment. "What should we do?"

"Surprise is better."

"What?"

"Surprise. We go storming into Ike on the warpath, and we're going to have to kill everyone."

"That would be Chaos."

"Yeah, yeah. I don't give a shit about that, but there's an awful lot of people in there. Close quarters—works to our advantage, but the place looks like a maze. Could get trapped and have to kill everyone anyway. No, I say we go through with this... quest... get on their good side. Then, we hack our way to Cheatums."

"And Beatums," Vagine added.

"Yeah, yeah. Sure, kid."

"So onto Alma?" Ajax asked.

The comedian nodded as he re-sheathed Side-Splitter on his back. "Let's make it quick. If there's one thing I know about Cheatums, he's hard to pin down. Right now, we know where he is. By the time we get back, he might be the regional manager. He has that way about him."

"I like this plan. It is the Good plan. You're doing the right thing."

"Oh, gross. Don't. Just don't," the comedian said as he turned and walked away from the two women.

Can't take a compliment? Oddrey asked.

"A compliment from one of them is like a compliment from a dog. It doesn't know any better. Because you can turn doorknobs and wipe your own ass, it thinks you're a God. A dog's compliment isn't worth a split bean."

You're doing the right thing, Oddrey said.

But the comedian didn't think he was. A part of him, the part that had kept him alive for the last however many years, wanted him to turn back around, head into Ike and rain down death and destruction on everyone. That would be the right thing to do. After all, what was right for one was wrong for others. Just because his plan might be good for the poor customers of Ike, didn't mean it was good for him. If Cheatums slipped through his fingers once more, he would lose his mind.

Isn't it already lost? Oddrey said.

"Don't you start in on me as well."

Behind him, Ajax and Vagine walked, listening to a one-sided conversation. Vagine looked at Ajax, her eyebrows raised. Ajax took her index finger, pointed it at her temple and swirled it around a bit. Vagine nodded as the comedian trod on, speaking to Oddrey and trading barbs.

Chapter 5: The People of Alma

The path wound through typical wasteland fare.
Though there was far more green here than on the journey
to Ike, it was still not what one would consider lush. Sparse
stands of weedy plants jutted up into the sky, looking like
spaceships ready to launch into the air, their yellow
blossoms leaking clear fluid upon the dry soil, and each of
them inherently knew to walk around the plants. Small
handfuls of grass stood waving at them periodically.

The only other trouble they had, besides the ever-
present, burning sun, came in the form of a faint echo of
sound off in the distance. The comedian and his
companions, like two ankle-weights locked to his legs,
stopped and listened.

"Purrthquake," the comedian whispered. They stood
that way, listening to the sound of thousands of pattering
little paws stampeding across the wastes. Eventually, after
about twenty minutes or so, the sound faded away, and they
continued their journey through the snaking path, moving
silently, aware there could be things out there worse than
gigantic tumbleweed balls.

At one point, they chanced upon an intersection, the
pavement ending some thirty feet away from a few burned-
out hulks of cars, as if someone had come along and cut
away all the road around it. If you stood there and tried to
figure out how this random road had been transported to the
middle of nowhere, you could go mad. The hulks, ancient
and rusted, the tires eaten away by sun, wind, and heat,
seemed like something from long ago, the type of stuff an
archeologist might unearth after months of digging.

"What are they?" Vagine asked.

"Cars," Ajax said.

"Cars?"

"There used to be millions of them."

"Millions?"

"A lot."

"They used to take people places, driving five times faster than a person could run. On roads, there would be so many of them that it would look like a sea of cars stretching into infinity."

"Sea?"

The comedian had had enough. "Oh, Jayzus. Look! That's the sun!" he screamed pointing to the sky. "That's the earth! These are hands," he said, wiggling his fingers around.

Ajax frowned at him, and the comedian stopped his ranting. "Don't mind him," she said. "He knows everything and thinks everyone else should as well."

"Is he a god?"

A brief snort of amusement escaped Ajax's lips. "Not by a long shot."

Onward they walked, the comedian annoyed by the basic chatter behind him. Sweat coursed down his face, and he had to lift his goggles off several times to clear the fogging insides. By the time a large square building rose up before them, he'd had thoroughly enough of Vagine. He would be happy to leave her in Alma. He wouldn't need her anymore, and they could move faster without someone bleeding from the foot. Besides, she'd be better off in Alma, whatever the hell it was, although, as the building loomed up ahead of them, he knew exactly what it was.

The building stood large and blocky, just like Ike. When the regional manager had called it competition, he had thought it just a turn of phrase, a holdover expression from the Old World. But, in the Old World, his world, where people had gone to megastores to fulfill all their needs, Alma had been known as Walmart. A few of the letters on the side of the building were missing, but for the middle four letters. There, floating at the end of the word, hung the yellow sunburst pattern, their logo—a symbol that looked like nothing more than Big Bird's balloon knot.

Creepers climbed the side of the building, wavering back and forth, as if the earth itself was trying to eat the structure. Shopping carts rusted on the apron of parking lot surrounding the store, and outside, a couple of dim children raced along, pushing each other back and forth in a shopping cart, running as fast as they could until the cart hit waste sand and tipped over, launching the children into the air. A fun game. Stupid but fun.

As they emerged from the crack of the valley and set foot on the apron of concrete, the children looked up, screamed as one, and ran for the safety of Alma. The comedian didn't care. Let them run and tell. They were here for one thing and one thing only—to find… *Fuck, I forgot the name.*

"What was that guy's name again?" the comedian asked.

"Klampenborg."

"Right. Klamberg. Got it."

Vagine and Ajax shared a look, silently acknowledging just how terrible the comedian was with names. And then they strode right up to the front doors of Alma where a person in a blue vest greeted them.

"Hello! How are you today?"

The person speaking to him was of indistinguishable sex. One of the person's eyes… *hung* for a lack of a better word, almost as if their face was melting. The other eye was cloudy and appeared to be looking off into the distance. Sores pocked their face, and in their hand, they clutched a roll of smiley face stickers.

"Oh, pretty good, you know. Just got attacked by a violent ball of tumbleweeds, but we're still here." The comedian was in full performance mode now, his winning smile on full display, though he didn't know if the person across from him could even see.

"Anything you're looking for today?"

"Yeah, I'm looking for a man named Klamberg."

"Klampenborg," Ajax corrected.

"Oh, we have all sorts of people inside. Don't know all their names, but I'm sure you can find a Klampenborg or a Klamberg, whichever you wish. Would you like a sticker?"

"No," the comedian stated.

"Of course," Ajax said.

The greeter plucked at the roll, dirty jagged fingernails scrabbling at the shiny roll of paper. Finally, they were able to pluck a sticker free, and with their filthy hand, they reached out and pressed the sticker to Ajax's chest. The comedian shuddered at the sight of contact between the two.

"And what about you?" the person asked Vagine, their head looking in the wrong direction.

The girl nodded her head, and the greeter repeated the process. With that done, they stepped inside the building, out of the sun and into the cool shade. Of course, the comedian would have traded the coolness for a bit of fresh air. The inside of Alma smelled like a combination of sour milk, extreme body odor, and fecal matter. It wasn't too hard to see why.

All over the store, people milled about, twisted people, weirdos, muties, melted folk.

"Don't touch anything," the comedian said.

Ajax's face was pale, like she was on the verge of throwing up. She asked, "Where do we start?"

"I guess we just start asking people, right?"

The first person the comedian approached was a mountain of a man with the face of a fetus. Scraggly patches of hair stood out on his head. His face was bulbous, childlike, the lips too red, too plump in his pale, colorless face. His eyes were multicolored things, slate, green, brown, and black, the pupils uneven circles.

94

"Do you know a Klampenborg?"

"Who dat, fam?"

The comedian looked over his shoulder and shook his head at the others.

"Klampenborg. He's a man."

"No cap. Truss bra. Lotta dem in da 'Ma."

The comedian was getting nowhere. The giant baby man turned away from them, digging in his ass.

"Did any of you understand that?" the comedian asked.

Ajax shook her head.

Vagine though seemed confused. "You didn't get it?"

"Sounded like a bunch of nonsense to me."

"Um…" Vagine looked at the rafters, thankfully free of people, and tapped on her chin. "He said there's a buncha men in Alma."

The comedian sighed. This was going to take forever, especially if he had to rely on Vagine to translate.

"Maybe this place has a manager too," Ajax supplied.

Another of the people of Alma squatted in the aisle and relieved herself on the tiles. She stood, her bare back dripping with sores, the pus the consistency of undercooked egg yolk. "Clean up on aisle ten, fam. How bout dat!" She giggled, hiking up a filthy, brown diaper and ran down the aisle.

"Holy smokes," the comedian said. "This place is a madhouse… a madhouse."

"What's wrong with them?" Ajax asked.

Vagine shrugged her shoulders. "Seem on da reg ta me."

Together, the three huddled close as they wandered the aisles. The city of Alma was huge, its insides cordoned off by rack after empty rack. The people of Alma, large, twisted, and barely able to be considered human, roamed the aisles, picking up random items from the sparse racks, playing with them, and then tossing them back onto the metal with a clang. None of the Almans seemed concerned to see them there. In fact, they were so busy "shopping" that the trio passed unnoticed in most cases.

A man with three rolls of fat on his large, bald cranium bent over, his spotty diaper exposing copious amounts of asscrack. He grabbed an oft-beleaguered spatula and began spanking himself. "Yeah, fam! Get it bra!" another Alman yelled. Skinny, with a couple of extra sets of ribs in his elongated torso, the man pumped his fist in the air, an ancient Budweiser hat perched on his triangular head.

"One thing's for sure," the comedian said. "We need to find Clampers and get the hell out of here."

Ajax, who felt like crawling inside herself to get away from the revolting people of Alma, nodded her head and didn't even bother correcting the comedian. The comedian was good at a lot of things, but names didn't appear to be one of them.

What's wrong with them? Oddrey asked.

The comedian didn't know, but everywhere he looked, he saw slovenly people with all sorts of mutations, their faces simple, their bodies covered in their own filth. The aisles themselves were more akin to a sewer than a walking path. When he left Alma, he would spend the first ten minutes of his freedom from the stench of the town wiping his boots in the waste dust.

"You know Clambarge, right Vagine?"

Vagine nodded, her eyes wide. If anything, she seemed as put off by the people as Ajax did. She probably wasn't as accepting as he himself was. The comedian had seen places like this, mostly on the outskirts of large cities, bubble towns where the DNA of the local populace had become ripped and shredded, creating all sorts of sad monstrosities. Seldom were the resulting mutants violent or

96

mean. If anything, they lived a pitiful life of derision at the hands of normies, of whom there seemed to be less and less each year.

But this place, Alma, was nowhere near a large city, unless he was way off in his head about their exact position in the world. If he had to pick out the location of Alma and Ike on an Old World map, he would put them somewhere in the lower part of Idaho. Although, given how the world was broken, they could be anywhere. Hell, while they slept, the spit of land they had slumbered on could have detached from the rest of the earth, hovered in the air and landed in some other part of the wasteland without them knowing. He wouldn't put it past the bitch—the planet that is.

They rounded the corner, and in the middle of a clearing, a massive orgy was taking place. The amount of drooling and oozing he saw was nothing compared to the stench.

"Uh, let's go the other way," the comedian said.

A man with two necks, one ending in a worthless stump yelled, "Get in on this, guvna. Plenny of holes still left, bra. Spill the tea, boo!"

"Nope. Not gonna happen," the comedian called, stalking away from the mound of twisted flesh and soiled diapers. For a second, Vagine stood rooted to the spot, and then Ajax grabbed her by the elbow and hustled her along.

Their boots clomped down another aisle, taking them out of sight of the revolting flesh mound. The deeper into the store they went, the darker it became. The smells were sharper as well. The comedian began climbing one of the racks, more as a method of getting some fresh air than as part of any actual plan.

Up he went, ignoring the scattered refuse of what was once a store full of goods. Empty tin cans, a DVD of the movie *Prayer of the Rollerboys*, and discarded price tags all slid by his eyes as he climbed up the metal rack, hoping it didn't tip over under his weight. As he climbed, the air grew thinner, the reek of flesh and excrement lessened. When finally he stood on top of the rack, he scanned the interior of Alma, studying the rows and the empty spaces between. There, at the back of the store, he spotted something that stood out. A booth set high up in the wall, a place for the manager to hang out, to observe the filth and fury without having to smell the aftermath. A light, dim and flickering, glowed within.

Fixing the location in his mind, he leaned over, peering down at Ajax and Vagine. The air between the aisles hung so thick he could see it, a faint brown haze hovering over everything. A lesser man would have gagged at the sight, but not the comedian, he threw up right then and there, tilting his head to the side so as not to spew on Ajax and Vagine. Feeling better, he wiped his mouth with the back of his arm and called down to the pair. "Get up here!" he yelled.

The two began climbing, and he stood staring at the gleaming light. The tops of the racks and the spaces in-between looked like nothing more than a huge maze. It was certainly not the layout the store had originally been designed with. It was confusing, purposefully, and as he studied the labyrinth, he realized that if they had kept walking between the racks, among the twisted, disgusting, pathetic people of Alma, they never would have found their way to the office. Where the doors to the storerooms and offices should be, the racks formed a solid line, unbreakable and impenetrable but from above.

Ajax stood nervously on the top of the rack, her arms out to her sides as her hips popped in and out as she tried to maintain her balance.

"You're not afraid of heights, are ya?"

"Afraid, no. But my head goes swimmy."

"Well, there goes the acrobat show I was planning. Guess you'll have to stick to being The Human Target."

98

Ajax did not look amused. Vagine, probably too stupid to be scared, walked along the top of the rack without any reservations. Dumb people were capable of amazing feats of bravery... or stupidity depending on how you looked at it.

"Come on," the comedian called.

He was in a good mood. The quest was going better than expected. He hadn't had to expend much energy getting here, hadn't lost any gear, and was looking to get the thing over in a day or two. Not bad for a quest. Of course, at the end of this quest, he was going to break open Ike, cut it in two, and let the wastes pick out the insides like a seagull with a crab in its beak.

They hustled across the top of the racks, occasionally hopping over random crap discarded on the top shelves. Of the Almans, they saw nothing but what they beheld in the gutters. That's what the comedian called the spaces below the racks. It seemed the people of Alma were too stupid to realize they could be above the wretched floor... or that they could leave completely. The comedian didn't know why anyone would want to stay in a place like this.

They have each other, Oddrey proposed.

"Gross. Don't be so damned optimistic, Odd. It's not a good look on you."

Maybe you should put them all out of their misery.

"Now that's too dark. See if you can dwell in the middle, like me.

They stink like shit.

"Now you're talkin'. Even keel, Odd. Even keel."

Onward they ran, occasionally forced to climb down and back up again, each time exposing themselves to more dimwitted debauchery, more filth. As they wended their way deeper into the store, the smell grew stronger, until the comedian was forced to pull his begging bandana, a faded, tie-dyed thing, from his back pocket. Once it was secured over his nose and mouth, it helped—a little.

Eventually, they reached the edge of the labyrinth, looked down over the edge of the metal rack and discovered nothing but darkness and blank store floor.

"Let's keep it quiet," the comedian said. "No more chatter."

"We're not the ones who have been talking," Ajax said, casting an accusatory glance his way.

"Uh, whatever." With that, the comedian descended the rack and stepped into the blackness below. His boots, covered in filth, squelched and slipped upon the dusty linoleum. He pulled Rib-Tickler free, his trusty blade, covered in snake poison and the blood of… of a snake, and he stalked quietly into the narrow alley of shadow between the metal rack and the back wall of Alma.

They creeped along, heel to toe, heel to toe, moving agonizingly slow. The comedian didn't want any surprises. He wanted to *be* the surprise. In the gloom, he spotted a rectangle of black. Two double-doors, closed and sealed. When he shoved on them, they refused to budge. He jammed the blade of Rib-Tickler between the two doors, feeling around until he managed to slip the blade between the latch that kept the doors closed. Prying with his knife, he inched the doors open until he could get his ungloved fingertips around the edge. He pulled and stepped aside, letting the others through. Once they were in, he turned and closed the door as softly and quietly as he could, though there was still a small, metallic click as the door latched closed once more.

The musty, dusty smell of old cardboard made the comedian's nose tingle in the complete darkness. "Gimme a sec," he whispered. In the quiet, he could hear Vagine and Ajax breathing. Reaching into his bag, he pulled a cord free and plugged the end of his rope lights into it. Instantly, a dim brightness filled the space, emanating from the rope

100

lights strung around the comedian's chest. Boxes stood piled high all around them, row after row of unopened treasures stacked as high as the ceiling would go. On the ground level, many of the boxes were open, tossed to the side, but the ones higher up were untouched.

"Woooow!" Vagine whispered.

"Shut up," the comedian hissed, louder than Vagine had initially spoken.

Her mouth snapped shut. Off to their right, he found what he was looking for. Though he wanted to sit and go through the boxes of the storeroom, spend an entire day pulling them off shelves and opening them up like a kid at Christmas, it was the stairwell he looked for. He had a quest to complete, after all.

The stairwell he found was a rickety thing. Once composed of solid lumber, it creaked and cracked as he tested out each step. There was no way around it. Sometimes the best alarm system in the world was a rickety set of stairs. He would lose the element of surprise in going up the steps. He'd have to be ready.

"Be ready for anything," he told Ajax. "Vagsjon, you stay here in case anything happens."

"You said my name right."

"Yeah, yeah. Don't get all teary eyed about it." With that said, the comedian took a few deep breaths, pulled Last Laugh, his shuriken, free from his jacket and held it between his teeth. In his left hand, he held Rib-Tickler, Side-Splitter being too large and unwieldy in the close confines of Alma's warehouse. Up the stairs he went, walking as softly as he could, though every step brought a creak. At the top of the stairwell, he stood in front of the metal door set perfectly within its frame. He reached for the doorknob. Silver and cold against the flesh of his bare fingers, the knob did not turn.

"Shit," he hissed.

He glanced back at Ajax, who stood below him on the steps. Her green eyes twinkled in the illumination of his rope lights. "Get Vagine up here," he hissed.

Ajax disappeared, somehow not making a single sound as she descended the steps. When she came back, Vagine stood wide-eyed and frightened next to her. The comedian could tell by the red in her eyes she had been crying.

Aw, you made a friend, Oddrey mocked.

"Vagine, I want you to call whoever's in here. Get 'em to open the door. Can you do that? Can you speak like those things out there?"

"Truss," Vagine said.

"What the fuck does that mean?"

"Yes."

The comedian waddled around on the landing so Vagine could stand next to the door. Standing this close to her was more bearable than the stench in the aisles, but only barely. What followed was a stream of nonsense the comedian couldn't hope to decipher. Waste-speak, an evolution of the language, or devolution depending on how you looked at it. Vagine's lips rose and fell, sneering as she garbled up the English language, turning it into a mockery of itself. The sheer stupidity of the words coming out of her mouth enraged the comedian, and when finally, the door pulled open, he had no need to get himself pumped. With Last Laugh gripped between his teeth, and Rib-Tickler in his hand, he rushed the door, sending the person on the other side flying backward.

A woman, old and gray, landed on her back, her hands up in supplication. "Please, don't kill me!" she called.

She said, "please," Oddrey giggled.

The comedian stood over the woman, scanning the small office for threats. Seeing none, he relaxed a bit, but only long enough to slip Last Laugh from his mouth and back into his jacket pocket.

102

In the dim light, he studied the woman. Her brown skin was smooth, despite the wrinkles on her face, and as he studied her skin, he felt something not quite right about it, something eerie and unnatural. The woman scrambled backward awkwardly, attempting to hide her face with her long gray hair.

"Who are you?" the comedian asked, his suspicions beginning to grow.

"I am the m-m-manager," she stammered, though there was something odd in the stammer. Something... artificial.

Another question popped into his mind. "What are you?" he asked.

"I am the m-m-manager," she repeated.

Her words came out in the same exact tone and pitch, so perfectly repeated that the comedian felt like he was watching a replay of reality versus talking to an actual human being. His hand tensed on Rib-Tickler, and he resisted the urge to stab it into her guts.

"You're not human," he said.

At this, the manager stopped trying to hide her face. She let her gray hair hang and looked up at the comedian. Her eyes were bright, unnatural things, the skin of her face was smooth, too smooth, the wrinkles etched into her plastic-y skin too perfect to be natural. The comedian bent down and poked the manager's cheek while she stared defiantly at him. The skin lacked the elasticity of actual human skin. It looked normal enough, somehow slightly off, but normal enough. But the feel was anything but ordinary.

"Again, I ask, what are you?"

"I am the m-m-manager."

"Say that again, and I'll cut you open from bits to breather. See what's inside." The comedian, not the most social of people in the best of times, had little patience for the artificial, and this "manager" was as artificial as they came.

"What are you doing?" Ajax whispered.

"Touch her," the comedian told her.

Ajax did as she was told and bent down to touch the ancient figure. She snatched her hand away as if she had been shocked. "It feels weird."

"That's because she's not human. She's a fuckin robot."

"Robot?"

"A machine. She's all bolts and gears inside."

"Why would someone make such a thing?"

"Gross, right?"

The manager glared at them. "I am not gross. I am the m-m-"

"M-m-m-manager. We got it, alright, lady? You can stop saying it. And by the way, from where we're standing, it doesn't look like you manage shit. Have you seen what's going on down there?"

"May I stand?"

"No, you may fucking not."

The manager harrumphed, a very solid facsimile of an annoyed human. "Do not question my management style. You might question anything, but not that. I have within me the memories and the experiences of over two-thousand managers. I know more about leading a store than anyone in the world most likely."

The comedian shook his head. "Lady, that's not a store anymore."

"It is a store. A very successful store. The customers are happy, and that's what is most important."

"Happy?" Ajax spat, her disgust apparent. "They're rolling in their own shit down there."

The manager looked at Ajax, blinking. The comedian thought he heard the sound of little motors clicking on and off as she did so.

104

"It's not my job to tell customers what should make them happy. The customer is always right, and in this case, they have exactly what they want. Enough food to live. Enough debauchery and entertainment to keep them happy."

The comedian sat on a cardboard box in the corner. He put his knife away, slid it home in its scabbard. "How did this happen?"

The manager grew more relaxed now that the comedian's knife was away. She glanced at Ajax and said, "I will not harm you. You are potential customers. The customer is always right."

Ajax slid the Holiest of Holys into her belt and stood with her arms folded. Vagine stooped behind Ajax's back, peeking out from the side every now and then. She had a healthy respect for managers, as she should.

"I will tell you the story of my store, and mayhaps you will want to stay. I see assistant manager material in the two of you. I also have a couple of security positions open."

Ajax and the comedian shared a bewildered look.

"I have been manager of this store for close to s-s-sixty years, or th-th-thirty. It is not clear. The data I have is conflicting. Internal clocks appear to re-re-reset themselves every so often. This store was once the crown jewel of the corporation, the future of retail. As you have sur-surmised, I am an artificial lifeform, specifically, a cutting-edge human resources management device. I have been infused with more s-s-store knowledge than a thousand human managers could ever hope to contain within their puny little brains. No offense, humans."

"None taken," the comedian said.

You're definitely offended, Oddrey said.

"Shut up, Odd."

The manager cocked her head to the side, and this time, the comedian definitely heard little motors whirring about in her neck. "Curious. Potential applicant number one appears to be speaking to something invisible. Noted. Application still a-a-active, interview ongoing." The manager's head returned to its normal upright position with a small *whirr*.

As if the manager hadn't just spoken her thoughts out loud, she continued onward. "I was to be the future, the first of my kind. The labor shortage, the rampant absences due to illness, all these things sought to bring down the corporation, but this they would not have. So they invented me. I am the u-u-ultimate employee. I don't need breaks. I show up to work every day. I don't need benefits because I don't get sick. I don't fall for the sob stories of other employees. *Oh, my m-m-mother died, can I have the week off?* You can have the rest of your life off. As you can see, I am the perfect manager."

"Yeah, perfectly inhuman," the comedian added.

"You see it as a fault to be inhuman, but look at what your kind has wrought on the world. It wasn't the m-m-machines that did this. It wasn't me who dropped b-b-bombs, invented new viruses, and sucked the world dry of its natural resources until it couldn't stand it anymore. It was humans. I am the solution to the ultimate problem, h-h-humanity."

The comedian nodded knowingly. "See, I knew it. Human-hater. Gonna try and destroy humanity."

The manager laughed then, as hideous a sound as he had ever heard. He doubted whoever had programmed the manager had programmed her to sound like that. Instead of typical laughter, a series of loud clicks and pneumatic exhalations escaped from the manager's throat. When she was done, she said, "Silly applicant. Humanity is fully capable of d-d-destroying itself without my interference."

The comedian shrugged. *She's not wrong.*

"Look," the manager beckoned, pointing to the office's window. "Down below, humanity is carrying out its final e-e-endgame. Soon, the people below will be incapable of doing anything about their world, about their plight. Even now, they refuse to leave the store. They are happy customers, and as with all perfectly happy things, they lack innovation. Even their cells, their sperm and their eggs, lack the ability to innovate, so they devolve, return back to the simplicity of their natural state. Gone are the self-destructive whims, the need to create and leave their blighted marks upon the world. They just want to eat and f-f-fornicate, and eat while they fornicate. Soon, they'll be too stupid to even f-f-fornicate. Even now, they have trouble reproducing, though it still happens."

"I was one of you," Vagine said meekly from behind the protective barrier of Ajax.

The manager focused on the meek girl, metallic things clicking and clanking in her fake skull. "Yes, I recognize the facial structure. Why are you back here?"

"I came home."

"You are barren, an evolutionary dead-end. Your intelligence, though limited, is far too great for you to continue being a customer. There is no home for you here."

"But I have no place to go."

"Customers must have a p-p-purpose. They must pay for their goods. You have no function, no purpose, therefore you cannot pay. Buy or get out, those are the rules."

The comedian had heard enough. "You don't want to stay here Vagine. There's nothing for you here anyway." The comedian looked around the office, measuring it, and decided he had enough room. Unlimbering Side-Splitter, he stood from the cardboard box.

"What are you doing?" the manager asked.

"I'm freeing this place. Consider it a corporate takeover."

"You can't. The c-c-customers will die without me."

"Maybe," the comedian said, "but this little experiment of yours is over. Unless, you can tell me where Klampenborg is."

"Kl-kl-kl-ampenborg?" The manager's eyes stirred in her sockets, tracking from side to side faster than hummingbird wings. "Accessing data streams. Accessing visual logs."

The comedian stirred his fingers in a circle, urging the manager to hurry up.

"Klampenborg, yes. New customer. Appeared one week ago. Now in aisle three—toys."

"Thank you," the comedian said. Then he swung Side-Splitter, severing the android manager's head with a shower of sparks and a burst of ozone. Her head sailed through the air and clanged off a wall as her robotic hands reached up to touch the wound. The fingers spasmed, accompanied by the sound of whirlygigs and whoziwhatsits spinning as they made their final turns.

"Application... d-d-denied," the manager's head managed to utter as the light faded from her inhuman eyes, her voice dwindling to a dying, electronic whisper.

"Why did you do that?" Ajax asked.

"It's better for everyone."

"But, these people." Ajax stalked over to the office window and peered out over the labyrinth of Alma. In the shadows, shapes moved, dark shapes, engaged in random entertainments and earthly pursuits. They walked on, never knowing someone watched over them. "They'll die without the manager."

The comedian came to stand next to her. "They'd die with her as well. At least now, they will learn something of what it is to be human, and when the food runs out, they may step into the light, find they like the feel of the sun on their faces and the earth beneath their feet."

"But some of them won't."

"True."

108

"A death sentence then."

"We've all been sentenced to death. Some of us just choose to find it sooner."

Ajax chewed over the comedian's words, weighing his madness and brokenness in the grand scheme of things. She didn't disagree with the comedian's assessment. Certainly, the manager had to go. It was an abomination, a freak. Such things needed to be put in order. But to take the head off the snake and leave the body thrashing in the labyrinth below, well, she didn't know if that was the right move. *Where he goes, Chaos. Where he treads, Blood. Only until the Broken Man is mended will the cycle cease.*

Ajax sighed. She had more work to do. For the past few days, she had believed she was making progress, that through her continued presence and encouragement, the comedian was making ground. But here again was another settlement destroyed by the comedian's mere presence, his whim, his will. The Broken Man had broken again. She didn't know how much more of this she could take.

"Well, who wants to check out some toys?" the comedian asked, all smiles.

Maybe we can find me a body, Oddrey said.

"Yeah, maybe."

You don't sound hopeful.

"Bodies are good. We'll keep an eye out."

Ajax turned and wondered what the comedian had meant by his last words. *Bodies are good? He's more broken than I thought.*

****

The comedian strode happily down the stairs, his boots clomping down the creaking wood. He had a bounce in his step now. The hard part was over. He had a location for Klampenborg. Just had to grab the silver and get the hell out of here, and it was all good. But first, he had to see.

109

In the warehouse, he pushed a tall, rolling staircase against one of the shelves lined with boxes. The metal steps rang underneath his feet. At the top, he shoved box after box to the ground, not even giving a warning to Ajax and Vagine. If they didn't know to get the fuck out of the way, that was their problem.

The boxes were heavy, and when they tumbled to the ground, they split open, spilling their contents all over the place. More boxes came down, more broke open. When the comedian finally clambered down from the staircase, he stood among piles and piles of metallic objects.

"What are they?" Vagine asked.

"Bad news," the comedian said.

"We can't leave this stuff for them," Ajax said.

The comedian swiped a hand across his forehead. At his feet, dozens of assault rifles and boxes of ammunition lay spread all over the warehouse floor. "Shit."

"But… what are they?" Vagine asked again.

"Guns. With an armory like this, those Almans could change the face of the wastes. Destroy everything in their path. Disgusting." The comedian turned to Ajax. "You know how to disassemble these?"

Ajax had seen guns before, old things hanging on the walls of The Coop, rusting in the waste air. The bullets had all been used up. They were now just decorations, a memorial to the pain they had caused. In the early days of her education, she and her friends had been given a firearms course, and they had been taught to disassemble and clean all types of guns. As the years went on, and working guns had faded away, The Coop had cancelled the class. "Yeah. I can figure it out," she said.

"Good. Take these apart, pull all the firing pins. We don't need a bunch of these droolers running around with weapons out there. When you're done with that load, search the boxes up there, see if there are anymore."

"What are you going to do?" Ajax asked.

"I'm gonna find Clambake."

Ajax nodded and plucked a rifle off the floor, fumbling about with it, trying to discover the trick of pulling it apart.

The comedian slapped Vagine on her arm, immediately regretting it and wiping his hand on his military jacket. "You're with me."

Vagine nodded.

****

Back in the foul air of the store proper, they clambered over the metal shelves. In the faint light, they could just make out the numbers on the ends of the racks, though they weren't arranged in any particular order. They must have been moved dozens, if not hundreds, of times over the years. Running along the tops of the racks, they beheld sight after sight of slobbering simplicity. Orgies, fights, freestyle rapping and beatboxing—they saw it all.

Looks fun, Oddrey said.

"Yeah, if you have the mind of a hamster, it might be."

Over the tops of the racks they flew, leaping from one to the next, scanning the end caps for numbers as they went. *187, 34, 56, 1...* the numbers flew by.

Eventually, on the outer edge of the wall, they came to a place with a large gathering of Almans. They stood waiting patiently in line, and the comedian watched as, one-by-one, the people lined up to take their turn placing their lips next to the pipe. When they turned a spigot, brown, sludgy liquid poured out, spraying them in the face while they slurped up as much of the sludge as they could. When an Alman had their fill, they would wipe their face with the back of their hand, and stride away. Then the next Alman would step up to the spigot to consume their fill.

"What is that stuff?" Vagine asked.

111

"No fucking clue. But if it makes you like them, I'd suggest you stay away from it."

They ran on and on, hopping and leaping and climbing, all the while gagging on the stench of the diapered masses. Eventually, they came to aisle thirty-three, and the comedian skidded to a stop in his tracks. This aisle was pristine, untouched. All along it sat row after row of mainstream books. Nonfiction, fiction, hardback, paperback; piles of books sat on their racks, their covers and jackets collecting years' worth of dust.

"What are those?" Vagine asked.

"Books."

Vagine looked confused.

"You read them."

No change in her facial expression. "Are they dangerous?"

"Oh, they are deadly."

"Should we destroy them?"

"It's a treasure unlike any other. Perhaps when the Almans are gone, when their food runs out, someone will return here in a hundred years, maybe two-hundred, pick up those books and actually learn something. But then again, I see a bunch of James Patterson down there, so probably not. Let's go."

Onward they went, and not once did a single Alman look up. They had been trained to keep their eyes on what was in front of them, the shiny things on the racks, the bulbous, rounded bits of their bodies. The sky was nothing to them, an unchanging slate of blandness. Incapable of imagining the possibilities, of turning on their brains and creating new realities, they plodded on and on, locked between the spaces in the aisles. A more pitiful sight the comedian had never seen.

After an interminable time among the stench and the buzz of the Almans, they found the toy aisle, the shelves bare, but for a few children wandering its emptiness, and one man sitting on a lower rack, his head in his hands.

"That's him," Vagine said, "Klampenborg."

The comedian nodded, leapt from the top of the rack and crashed down with a squish and an awkward slip into the filth between the aisles. "Klampenborg!" the comedian called out, his voice challenging and loud.

The man started. His face was long, his mouth sagged open, the bottom row of his teeth packed in tight and crooked. There were too many teeth in there. His eyes were dim but held more of a luster than the Almans proper, and when the comedian called his name, he sat still and patient instead of fleeing like a cockroach as the comedian had expected. The man showed no aggression, just a dejection marked by a stooped back and sodden eyes.

"They sent yuz fer me, ya?"

The comedian nodded.

"Spose they be wantin' dis."

As Klampenborg reached behind his back, the comedian's hand went to Rib-Tickler sheathed on his leg. He needn't have bothered. In his hand, Klampenborg held it, the fabled brick of silver, which was really not a brick of silver.

"I dunna even know what tis," Klampenborg said. "Jus knows de bossmang like it."

Behind them, Vagine made a horrendous amount of noise as she climbed down the rack.

"Vagsjon! What are yuz doing here?"

"Me hep," she said, sliding into the Alman accent.

"Whyfer ya, hep? We same."

"Fer like. I hep fer like."

"Dissun?" Klampenborg asked, pointing at the comedian, who stood off to the side, trying to piece together the strange speech of the two wasters.

"Ach. Dead ass no."

113

"Tevs, tevs. Ya here to slay, poor ole, Klampenborg? Ya gon yellershirt me?"

The comedian turned to Vagine, an eyebrow raised. "He asks if you're here to kill him."

"All I need is the brick."

"Haves it den," the poor man said, thrusting the brick out to the comedian. "I've no use fer it." The comedian promptly grabbed it and stuffed it in his backpack.

"Why go?" Vagine asked.

"You wuz a babby when the yellershirts took us. I's this many." The man held up two filthy hands, all the fingers spread out. "I 'membered likin' Alma better. Membered goofin' in mud and seein' fun. I misses it, but Alma not de same. Sad place dis, tear-makin fuh me. Truss. Now, I got nowhere. Me's thinkin' I could trade da silva, be big man. But dees peeps, not even peeps. Manimals. Somehow badder den yellershirts. Now I's stuck. No place ta go. Kill me fer sure dey would."

The comedian was over the conversation. Some might find it interesting, but not him. He had what he'd come for.

"You comin'?" the comedian asked Vagine.

She turned to him, her eyes wide, her body covered in filth, and he saw a spark of something in those eyes. "Klampenborg's right. We no can go back. De yeller shirts would yellershirt us. I stay."

The comedian turned his back. "Yeah, whatever." With that he began climbing the racks.

"Tell Beatums… tell Beatums, I like him, whole lots. Maybe he'll come to me."

The comedian strode on, happy to be done with Vagine, and Klampenborg, whose grasp of the English language had been giving him a headache.

You're not even going to say goodbye? Oddrey asked.

"Why?"

Just to do it, like everyone else does?

"Me and you, we're not like everyone else. Don't forget it."

Oddrey fell silent, and for a moment, the comedian thought maybe he'd made a mistake. Maybe he could have talked Vagine into coming along with them. *But what the fuck would I want with Vagine?* Either way, it was too late to turn back now. Once the comedian made up his mind to go, there was no stopping him. Once his course was set, nothing could get in his way. In half a day, Cheatums was going to find that out. Still, a small part of him felt bad for not saying goodbye.

Chapter 6: The Return to Ike

"Where's Vagsjon?" Ajax asked.

"She decided to stay," he said.

Ajax cocked an eyebrow at him.

"What? She did!" he said defensively.

"You didn't kill her?"

The comedian spread his arms wide. "You think I would kill Vagine?"

Ajax's silence spoke volumes. As Ajax pulled the firing pins from the rifles, the comedian climbed the racks, looking for more weapons. He hated guns. Though, in the early days, he had used them often, it wasn't by choice, merely a method of survival, an attempt to fight fire with fire. Guns were lazy, a necessity when bullets had been flying around all day, every day. Yeah, the early days of the world's death had been a shooty place, everyone taking shots at each other, taking what could be taken. No one wanted to work for life.

But now, most of that had all gone away. Oh, you might find the occasional waster with a working pistol every now and then, but they were few and far between. It wasn't like those early days where people just drove along roads in their soon-to-be extinct vehicles stitching houses with gunfire and firing them into the air for every stupid little thing. Now, anyone who held a gun with live ammunition in it was holding off for something, saving that last bullet for an emergency, or God forbid, the day when they just couldn't take the end of the world anymore. These days, the comedian figured, most people with a working firearm fell into the second category.

With the last box of weapons off the racks, the comedian climbed down and helped Ajax finish the job.

When they were done, they kicked the rifles off to the side. The comedian's backpack and Ajax's satchel hung heavy, filled with the one piece needed to make the rifles work. The people of Alma would be better off without guns.

Together they took one last stroll through Alma, climbing the racks and walking above the people like gods. And who was to say they weren't? Compared to the drooling simps and muties below, they were better. No doubt about it. Still, as they hit the ground and said goodbye to the Alman greeter, the comedian couldn't help feeling bad they hadn't stumbled across Vagine before they went. He would have liked to have said goodbye at least. She was a good person in a world full of bad ones. Not too bright, but good all the same.

I knew you'd miss her.

"Shut up, Odd."

Together, Ajax and the comedian stepped out into the sun, the comedian immediately pulling his goggles down over his eyes. "Well, here we go again."

"Hey," Ajax said.

"What?"

"You did it."

"Did what?"

"Left a town without killing anyone."

"Well, don't get used to it."

The comedian waved back at the simple kids playing in their shopping cart, launching each other into the soil of the wasteland.

"Cute kids," he said conversationally to Ajax. "You know, if it wasn't for the extra ears and misshapen heads."

Ajax said nothing.

****

On the path once more, Alma faded from sight, the vision of its blocky structure blotted out by towering valley hills.

117

Without Vagine, the way was quiet, and Ajax and the comedian fell into an easy rhythm, striding along, chewing up the miles while the sun overhead dipped low behind the hills, plunging them into shadow. With any luck, they would get back to Ike by nightfall.

For a second, the comedian could almost pretend he and Odd were alone again, out on the road, wandering and looking for someplace to do his show and score a little food. Those days had been simple, easy days, days where he played out the string of his life with no other worries other than the ever-present rumbling in his belly and the intrusion of thoughts and memories he didn't care for. The days were easy, the nights not so much.

Dreams, horrid little things, clutching cries from his subconscious, made every night a struggle. Many were the times where he would wake up covered in sweat and on the verge of screaming. Scanning the area around him, he'd look for hidden dangers. He wasn't afraid of dying, had done so a long time ago for all intents and purposes. Those days had been easy because he had lived as a zombie.

Now, walking alongside a woman seemingly born decades after he was but who was still his same age or near enough, he wondered if he was, in fact, alive at all. But the gray in his beard was proof he was still aging. From whispering wasters, he'd heard tell of a type of people in the wastes dosed with enough radiation to twist their DNA, turning off the kill switch that allowed a human to die naturally. On they went, continuing to shamble, even as their bodies turned into mounds of tumors, until they became twisted and hideous to behold. They called them Oldies. But the comedian was no Oldie. Though he had aged sparingly, if Ajax wasn't blowing smoke up his ass, he hadn't aged enough to be considered an Oldie. Just a little gray.

But then, there was Yokel, a man who at first sight had been nothing more than another faceless name in a

118

small wasteland outpost. He'd been around during the death of the world, and he looked no older than anyone else on this godforsaken planet. A smile came to his lips as he thought about the little man. As he had watched Yokel do his cinematist schtick, he'd felt a growing affection within, a blooming like and appreciation for the man. He hadn't felt that way since before he was married, since before his wife had given birth to... well, whatever, he hadn't felt it in a long time. Now here it was, a feeling of wanting to be around people. That had to be proof he was alive.

Along with Yokel, he also had the case of Ajax. Guilt was an emotion he had long thought burned out of his repertoire. His one evil act, meant to save, to prevent a life of hardship and pain, when he had killed his own... well, whatever. All he meant was that he thought he'd burned up all his guilt, used it all in one fell swoop. But, last night, in Ike, when Ajax had complained about him using her, he'd felt it—guilt for something other than the life-defining sin of his past.

That's a sign, right?

Oddrey giggled.

The comedian resented the change in his heart. Once, when he was a teenager, he'd had a vivid, knockdown, screaming-at-each-other argument with a friend in high school about Batman and Superman. The comedian had argued Batman was greater because he didn't need love, was capable of surviving without it. Superman was weak because he always had Lois Lane. His friend had argued that Superman's ability to love and keep relationships was his strength and what actually made him greater than Batman.

You're no Superman. Not even a Batman, Oddrey said.

The comedian didn't reply. It was obvious he wasn't a superhero. Superheroes didn't survive on the kindness of strangers and the things thrown at their friends. *Am I becoming weak? If I allow these people into my life, it can only lead to more heartache. I don't know if I can handle that.*

Ajax… there was an odd duck. Despite her constant threats to kill him, he found he was starting to feel something for her. Maybe it was like that movie where Tom Hanks became friends with a volleyball. *What was his name? Wilson.* At first, he had talked to the volleyball as a joke, and then, over time, he had become attached to it. Maybe that's what was going on with him and Ajax. Certainly, she had the personality of a piece of sports equipment, maybe a medicine ball with a face.

"Hey," he said.

"What?" Ajax asked as they passed through the mysterious crossroads, dead cars eyeing them with their busted-out headlights.

"I was thinking."

"That's a new one," Ajax said.

"Yeah, yeah. Anyway, I was thinking that if you wanted to learn how to actually juggle, I could teach you."

"Don't do me any favors."

The balls on this woman! The comedian fell silent. Inside he fumed. *That's what I get for extending an olive branch.*

Onward they walked, the comedian swearing in his mind, calling Ajax all sorts of names. Ajax just plowed on and on like a pack mule. She had all the conversational inertia of one of the mutie cactuses waving at them from the top of the valley, their needles twitching and jittering like a cat's tail.

Stupid Chicken Kicker. Thinks I'm broken. She's the one that's broken. Walking around with a doorknob on the end of a stick. Even her cloak is stupid. That green is hideous on her. And don't even get me started on the personality. It's like I'm hanging out with a rock all day. Can a person be born without a sense of humor?

120

As the comedian picked Ajax apart, broke her down into her loathsome pieces, she turned to him and said, "But I would like to learn."

And with that, all the pressure and hate the comedian had been building was released, escaping like the air from a balloon. "After our business is done in Ike, we will work on it."

Ajax nodded and on they strode.

Aw, you have a friend, Oddrey mocked.

"Shut up," the comedian whispered.

Are you trying not to look crazy in front of your friend? Aw, that's soooo sweeeet.

The comedian knew if he kept talking to Oddrey, she would just keep coming back with more mockery. Instead, he grunted his displeasure and let it drop. Onward they strode, the canyon walls drifting by with each dusty step.

The sun had disappeared entirely and they walked through deep shadows, gray streaks of burnt clouds drifting across the greening sky. *Ajax ain't so bad, I guess.*

****

Ajax plodded along, her hands stinking of old gun oil. Disassembling the rifles had been the right call, but she worried about what they were leaving behind in Alma. More Chaos she suspected. When their food ran out, what would Alma become? Another raider den, another place where life was cheap, and people killed each other at random? They could have fixed it, propped the town up and given it what it needed to thrive, but that would have taken time. And time was something the comedian didn't seem to have.

The enigmatic man was blind to everything else besides his driving need to finish his quest, to find this Cheatums, though she had no idea why he needed to find him. And after he found him what then? Would the comedian float through the wasteland like a leaf caught in the wind? Did he have a plan?

And what of Ike?

Ajax had seen the signs. It was a bad place, a place of Chaotic order. There was a system there, one many Chicken Kickers might shrug their shoulders at, point to the rules and laws and say, "They are following Order. They are paving the broken road." But Ajax wasn't so sure. They were eating people. Of that, Vagsjon had given them proof. While cannibalism wasn't expressly forbidden by the laws of The Coop, it was supposed to only take place in an emergency. If the choice was between dying and eating human meat, The Coop preferred their Chicken Kickers, their agents of Order, to stay alive. Dead Kickers paved no road.

But, on the other hand, Ajax saw a group of people being oppressed, being shoved down and used as a food source. Certainly, that needed to stop, but if they had broken no law, how was she to stop it? Her hands were tied.

But maybe… the comedian could… No. A Kicker is supposed to respond to the world, correct the wrongs, not maneuver people into doing wrong. You don't break the road even worse before paving it.

Locked in a moral conundrum she had no way of getting around, Ajax turned to the comedian and asked, "What is your plan for Ike?"

"Watch it," the comedian said, pointing off to her right. A lone tumbleweed charged at Ajax, and she batted it away with her mace.

They trudged on as if nothing had happened. The tumble weed rolled away, its course crooked and wobbling. A burnt breeze howled through the valley.

"I figure we go in there, give 'em what they want, and then ask to see Cheatums."

"And if they say no."

"We'll play it by ear."

"You're going to kill them all, aren't you?"

The comedian smiled at her, his perfect white teeth shining even in the shadowy gloom. "Ajax, I never go into a place planning to kill everyone."

"But it happens."

"I mean, you know, lots of things happen. Sun comes up. Sometimes it rains. Sometimes a tumbleweed tries to kill you. Things happen. Who can stop that? I know I can't."

Ajax swallowed, and then chose her next words carefully. "If they swing first, I will back you up."

The comedian nodded. And onward they trudged, Ajax wondering if she had compromised herself. She had promised Chaos, but only under certain circumstances. Was it a circumvention of her code? Maybe. But if it meant freeing Ike, and consequently Alma, from the hungry clutches of the yellow shirts and their regional manager, it might be worth it. Still, she had an uneasy feeling in the pit of her stomach.

"Watch it," she called to the comedian.

He pulled Side-Splitter free, swung it like a baseball bat and sent another tumbleweed trundling off into the distance, weaving its way among the rocks and scree.

With that taken care of, they continued their journey, listening for the sound of thundering paws as they neared Ike and the radglow of night overtook the sky.

Chapter 7: Ya Swedish?

Yokel spent his time lounging on the stage until a bunch of greasy wasters came to put it away. Quickly, Yokel snatched up the Fetus Grand off the ground, lest the workers, who seemed unconcerned with doing anything but tearing down the stage, damage it somehow. T.C. hadn't told him to look after the piano, but him and T.C. had a connection, and this connection told him the man would be furious with him if he let something happen to the piano.

In the town of Ike, a commotion built as it did every night. Once the radglow hit, the wasters kicked into high gear, moving around the store, transferring furniture from one place to another. Behind the shopping cart barricade, the scrape of furniture legs, the crash of metal on the ground, and the curses of the wasters was unending.

In the courtyard, Yokel sat, cross-legged, staring down the Long Natural Path, one hand resting protectively on the piano. He had been unable to see anything down the path, and his mind had grown more and more curious the longer he had been in Ike. Yokel sucked on his teeth, pulled out a chunk of something soft and pink and spat it on the floor. He was tired of eating protein fuel. The same thing every day. It was getting to him.

As the cacophony continued, Yokel sorted through his mental rolodex, looking for other movies he could play as a cinematist. As he was testing his knowledge of Police Academy movies, a figure appeared on the path. Low and shambling, Yokel recognized the form of the Lord of the Wrenches, Kallax.

Above, in the rafters, the people, their ankles tied to cords, dove down, wrapped their arms around furniture and dragged it into the air. Upon their second dip to the ground, they dropped the furniture in a new location. Watching them work made his head spin.

Kallax stood above him. "Greetings, cinematist."

"Greetings."

"May I sit?"

Yokel nodded, and Kallax collapsed to the concrete floor, flashing a couple of knobby knees in the process. He let out a great sigh as he straightened his robe, the Allen wrenches clinking and clanking underneath.

"You seem like a bright sort," Kallax muttered.

"Gee. Thanks." Such an utterance from anyone else would be seen as sarcasm, but from Yokel nothing more was transmitted other than utter gratitude.

"May I ask, if it's not too much trouble, what your heritage is?"

Yokel ran a hand through his hair, "I mean, I guess I would describe my hair as like, medium long, light brown. It's thick though."

Kallax's face wrinkled for a second before he regrouped and attempted a different tact. "No, no, not your hair. I mean, what is your nationality?"

"Well, I used to be American, but now, I don't know. Don't really have a home so much. I mean I did, but then old T.C. came, and then that was gone, so I guess I'm just a wanderer now."

Kallax started to get frustrated, though Yokel failed to pick up on it. His positivity was both a gift and a curse, in this case the latter. "What country were your forefathers from?"

"Well, I only had two fathers. But I had two mothers as well. I guess after being with each other my biological parents found out they were gay. You don't know how hard it is to grow up with four parents. Four people tellin' ya what to do. Four people screamin' at ya, tellin' ya not to watch The Love Guru. They were right, but what did I know? I was just a dumb little kid. I guess I shoulda listened. Worst movie of my life. Why, I swear, I didn't watch another movie for a whole 'nother month after that. Guess I was scared."

Kallax nodded through all this, the wrenches in his robe jingling with the movement, and then finally, when Yokel's diatribe against The Love Guru petered out, he asked. "Do you have any Scandinavian in you?"

Yokel patted his body down. "Who knows what's in me. I ain't never seen inside. Might be some Scandinavian in there, I guess. Whatever that is."

"Tell me, young Yokel, did you graduate high school, back before the bombs?"

"I went to it. But then I got the job at the theater, and they wanted me to work nights on account of I could clean and stuff because of my parents, but I wasn't uh, so good with the people. Lots of sweepin', sittin' in the projection booth. We used old projectors, you see."

Kallax tapped on his chin. "Did your parents, your blood parents ever say anything like, 'We're from Finland, or Norway, or Sweden? Hell, even Iceland?"

"Maybe. Cain't remember."

"But that's a definite maybe?"

"Maybe a definite maybe."

"Good enough." With that, Kallax waved his hand in the air.

"What're ya doin'?" Yokel asked, smiling like a goof. And then from above, a man came out of nowhere, wrapped his arms around him, and the next thing Yokel knew, he was flying through the air, his head spinning and that evening's protein fuel lurching in his stomach. The stench of the man holding him was too great, and it pushed him over the edge, pink vomit spraying from his mouth and splattering Kallax who looked up from far below.

He caught a brief image of Kallax swearing and wiping the pink goop out of his eyes, and then Yokel was twirling through the air again, free of the clutches of the rafterman who had grabbed him. Positive he was going to

126

plummet to his death among reasonably priced but not so durable furniture, he screamed. As he fell, beds and bookcases rushed up at him. Just before he was about to hit the ground, another set of stinking, filth-covered arms wrapped around his chest, and in this way, he was moved across the length of Ike, plucked out of the air before certain death at the very last second by rafterman after rafterman. They tossed him like a football in the days of yore. Eventually, poor Yokel could stand the terror no more, and he blacked out.

Chapter 8: Bust a Deal and Talk to the Home Office

They ran as fast as they could, hoping to make it to Ike before the thundering purrthquake rolled over them, stripping them of their flesh and blood. It was good Vagine had not come. She would not have made it on her injured foot.

Soon after the sun went down, about a mile away from their destination, they heard the tell-tale pitapat of thousands of paws. Bodies, sleek and lithe and wrapped in fur coats of orange, black, white, and tortoise shell, contracted and expanded as the cats hurtled across the valley floor, tumbling over each other and batting at each other occasionally. Their tails stood high and in excitement.

What fun it is to chase the hoomans.

"Shut up, Odd."

The ground rumbled around them, and dirt and rocks trickled down the sides of the valley walls at the approach of the purrthquake. In the greenness of the radglow, they saw the corner of the giant blue building of Ike looming up before them.

Gasping and exhausted, Ajax and the comedian put on a burst of speed. Without having to say anything, they both decided to put everything they had into their final sprint. There would be nothing left of them when they hit the doors of Ike, one way or another.

The comedian's thighs pumped like pistons as he lengthened his stride, the burning in his legs just one more indignity the waste had forced upon him. Add it to the list of sunburns, chapped lips, and ever-present thirst and hunger. The ground was treacherous in the deceiving evening. The radglow was a shifting light, and the stones on the ground seemed to writhe and twist under its glow, shadows pulsing and undulating underneath the angry green glare of the sky above. One wrong step and he would go down. *I'm too exhausted to get up again if I fall.*

Ajax, less encumbered than the comedian and with longer legs, shot ahead of him, propelling her way across the rocky ground. The comedian hurdled a boulder in his path, and then came down awkwardly on the other side, his ankle twisting within his boot. The pain was immediate, the fear of death springing up along with the pain. He limped onward as Ajax left him in the dust.

The sound of thundering paws drew closer as the comedian hit the concrete apron around the town of Ike. Lights glittered behind the dusty glass of the front doors, and the shadow of Ajax pounding on the glass made his heart leap in his chest. *Open the doors.*

Onward he ran, gasping for breath, cursing the weight of Side-Splitter on his back and all the bits and bobs in his many-pocketed jacket. The thought crossed his mind that he could ditch his gear, toss his backpack and his sword on the ground, but then he would have nothing to bargain with in Ike. And he knew a bargain was coming. They always wanted one more thing at the end of a quest, one more task. When someone in the wasteland knew you had something they wanted, this was always the way.

As the comedian approached the door, the hungry horde of felines on his coattails, he fully intended to plow through the glass. It was thick and strong, despite all the years. He might just bounce off it, but better to take the chance and perhaps live for another day than to face death by a thousand cat claws. He lowered his shoulder and his head, and then barreled into a couple of men in yellow shirts, tumbling to the smooth concrete floor of Ike.

The comedian disentangled himself from the arms and legs of the men on the ground and rushed to help Ajax close the doors. Pressing on the glass with his hands, the two slid the door closed just as the wave of cats broke over them. A handful of cats got inside as the door closed, and

129

then sat looking confused, their tails twitching. A chorus of plaintive meows went up from the cats, as they stared at Ajax and the comedian, waiting for the door to be opened once more.

The two hoomans shared a look, then opened the door a crack. The cats, imperious and demanding strolled out the door, and the two survivors sealed it up once more.

With that business settled, they turned and helped the yellow shirts off the ground. Before the yellow shirts were even on their feet, wasters streamed from the Long Natural Path and began working like a colony of industrious ants. Furniture scraped and skidded across the ground, the wasters working as one.

In front of Ajax and the comedian, the image of a courtroom began to take shape, with chairs and a juror's box formed from bookshelves tipped over on their sides. The judge's bench was built ridiculously high, and from the Long Natural Path, the regional manager appeared. On the backs of wasters who had transformed their bodies into a staircase, he ascended to his place, glaring down at the comedian and Ajax from behind the judge's bench.

The two companions stood in front of the judge as yellow shirts streamed out of the back of the town, their shopping cart shields affixed to their forearms.

Uh-oh, Oddrey said.

"Uh-oh indeed," the comedian echoed.

The regional manager, a well-fed looking individual, his skin glowing amongst the LED lights set up all around the town of Ike, spread his arms and welcomed them. "Our heroes return! Capable of putting on a show and getting a job done. You would have made fine employees indeed."

"Thank you, oh wise regional manager," the comedian began, trying to stave off the violence for a little bit at least, until he could catch his breath and judge the damage of his ankle properly.

"Have you been successful? Did you find the brick of silver?"

"Indeed, I did." The comedian made no move to produce it, instead stalling for time.

"And what of the traitor, Klampenborg, who failed to give his two-weeks' notice?" At this the wasters tssked and psshawed.

"He is dead as well." A few faces fell in the crowd, but not many. Death was a part of life now, not hidden behind mortuaries and morgues. Everyone here had seen hundreds of deaths, those alive during the fall of the world perhaps thousands.

The regional manager clapped his hands. "Outstanding! Truly employee of the month material. Am I right?" he called to his captive audience.

The crowd murmured, nodding their heads, a faint, semi-mocking golf clap doing the rounds amongst their number. The comedian got the feeling that to disagree with the regional manager would lead to more than a mere demotion. Despite her prohibition against lying, Ajax kept her mouth shut about Klampenborg, for once.

Maybe she's not as stupid as you think, Oddrey said.

"May we see the brick of silver?" the regional manager asked.

"First, terms," the comedian announced.

At this, the smile, that officious, bureaucratic smile, faded from the regional manager's lips, replaced by the scowl of a despot denied his right to anything and everything under the sun.

"Do you know who I am? I am the regional manager, and if I demand you to show me something, then you had best show it. The consequences of disobedience can be quite extreme."

The comedian watched the crowd lean in, hanging on every word. Surely the comedian would roll over at this. No one stood up to the regional manager—and lived that is.

131

"I am not an employee. I am a customer," the comedian announced. "We are customers," he said, pointing at Ajax and including her, for better or worse. "And the customer is always right."

At this the regional manager sputtered. "Insubordination!" the manager howled, and the crowd shrank back, the yellow shirts in the juror's box, readying the shopping cart shields on their forearms, pricking their fingers against the sharpened metal tines, preparing for a slaughter.

The comedian was ready for the regional manager's reaction. "It is not insubordination, for I am not your subordinate." A gasp went up from the crowd. The regional manager leaned forward, surprise on his face.

"Here now, waster. This is my land, my town, my region, and I am the manager of this store. There can be no one higher up than me. Tis impossible."

The comedian smiled. "I come from…"—dramatic pause—"the home office!" He pronounced this last as loudly as he could, and his voice echoed and boomed among the shitty furniture for all to hear, even in the back of the store. "I come undercover, checking up on you and the work you've done here, and I must say, this is as shoddy an operation as I've seen in some time."

"You have no right to say that!" the manager screamed.

"No right?" the comedian questioned. "Why look at your customers. Look at them. They're miserable, stupid, smelly. This is no way to treat customers."

"They are perfectly happy, fed and bred. What more is there?"

"They lack… life," the comedian responded.

"They breathe do they not?"

"Indeed."

"They shit, do they not?"

132

"Certainly," the comedian said, trying to avoid watching one waster doing just that on the Ikean floor.

"Then they are alive."

"It takes more than shitting and breathing to be happy," the comedian said. "A true human must need to better themselves, must be allowed to become whatever it is they want to be. Under you, these people are reduced to laborers, simpletons who move furniture about day after day. They are living breathing pallet jacks eating fetal glop to survive. That's not humanity. That's torture. And, on another note. Where the hell is my man, the cinematist?"

The regional manager, far from being cowed by the comedian's words, sneered down at them. "Give me the brick of silver, and you can have him back."

The comedian knew this conversation and this meeting could have gone any of a dozen ways, but all roads led to this confrontation. He had something the manager wanted, and the manager had something the comedian wanted. An impasse, tipped in the manager's favor by the human capital he commanded. But he was about to undo that, at least to some degree.

"Go fuck yourself. Under the power vested in me by the home office, your superiors, you are hereby relieved of duty. You're fired. Now get your ass out of here."

The regional manager sputtered, and the entire crowd sat wide-eyed, unsure of what to do.

The comedian continued. "The man or woman who brings me the manager's head shall be the next manager!"

The regional manager, not to be outdone yelled, "The customer who brings me the comedian's head, shall be my highest yellow shirt and assistant to the regional manager."

The people all around, confused, hit with wave after wave of stuff they didn't really understand, knew one thing. It was better to be in charge than not, and it really came down to proximity. Loyalties did not enter into the

133

equation. Those closer to the comedian, seeing an easier path headed in his direction. Those closer to the regional manager headed in his direction, and as soon as the first waster moved, the entire crowd kicked into action.

The comedian, ready for such an eventuality, unlimbered Side-Splitter. The blade glowed shining and deadly among the LED lights of Ike. As he tested his ankle, finding it merely sore, cries of "Bulla! Bulla!" went up from the crowd. Then they surged, trying to reach the regional manager and the comedian at the same time.

The first wave of wasters came at him, and though he didn't feel guilt per se, he definitely wasn't happy about mowing them down. His blade, heavy and sharp, ran through the mid-sections of three men like they were made of butter. Their hands, so recently balled into fists, snapped open and immediately went to their mid-sections to hold in their guts.

Then the battle was engaged fully, and skinny forms, greasy and stinky, swarmed about him, clutching and grabbing while the comedian performed his dance. It was not all that much different than when he performed on stage. The lights went on, and his mind, usually filled with pain, went somewhere else, disappeared completely as he focused on his movements, on his opponents. Side-Splitter lopped a man's head off, and before it even hit the ground, the comedian's sword was already blazing its way through another pile of flesh.

If the wasters had continued their press en masse, the comedian likely would have been overcome, but after the first wave of bodies hit the ground and the concrete floor of Ike became slick with the blood of their friends and loved ones, many of them backed off, disappearing into the maze of Ike, hiding amongst the furniture.

But still the tide came on, and more wasters breathed their last.

To his right, Ajax dueled a couple of yellow shirts who had thought her to be an easy mark. They must not have seen the show, because as they swung their shopping cart shields at her, she dodged them all, bringing the Holiest of Holys around to bash against their shields. They couldn't match her for long, and soon, their skulls were broken and their brains were different shapes in their skulls as their lifeblood poured from their heads.

As the fight continued, a new problem reared its ugly head, or better to say, "Lowered its head." An ear-piercing shriek, like that of an eagle, was all the warning the comedian had. When he glanced up, he spotted one of the raftermen descending, knives in his hands, plunging straight for the comedian. The comedian dropped to his knees, ducking the filthy mitt of a waster in the process. He leveled Side-Splitter upward, bracing the microphone pommel against the concrete. Like a pikeman awaiting the oncoming charge of cavalry, he allowed the rafterman to impale himself upon the blade. The rubber cord tied to the dying man's feet pulled him free, and he rebounded into the air, dripping blood like a partially bashed piñata losing its candy. All around them, droplets of the red stuff fell like rain.

Ajax, seeing the comedian on his knees, dispatched a group of wasters and moved to his back, blocking a strike that would have caved in the back of the comedian's skull. A yellow shirt, his face furious at being thwarted, turned and swung at her, the piercing tines of his shield aiming for her face. She ducked to the side, stepped inside his swing, and brought the head of her mace up under his chin. His jaw clacked together and then shattered entirely. A brutal hit for someone in the waste. Few people survived a broken jaw in this world, but the yellow shirt didn't have to worry. Ajax was filled with mercy, and she dropped the man to the ground permanently with a bash to the side of his skull.

The comedian's dance continued, as he balanced neutralizing the threat on the ground with keeping an eye out for more of the plunging raftermen. They hooted and hollered from above, jumping and leaping from rafter to rafter, their bungee cords in their hands, ready to be tied off for a dive from their lofty heights.

They'd make good acrobats if you could talk one into coming with you, Oddrey said.

"Not now, Odd."

Duck.

The comedian did as he was told. Oddrey had a good grasp of combat and frequently gave him directions, warned him of things he was only half aware of. As he ducked down, a forearm wielding a shopping cart shield swept over his head. When he turned to face his would-be assassin, the woman sneered at him and kicked him in the mid-section. The "oof" of exploded air from his body would have been comical at any other time, but he knew he was exposed at that moment. Side-Splitter fell from his hands, and the yellow shirt, seeing her opportunity, rushed in, the deadly tines of her shield aimed at the comedian's throat. But she never got there. Her arm fell before she could make contact, and when she looked down, she found Rib-Tickler sticking out of her ribs. It wasn't a killing blow by itself, but the poison on the blade ensured this yellow shirt's life was now at an end.

Looks like she's ready to take the Long Natural Path to hell, Oddrey crowed.

"Bulla, bulla," the comedian concurred. With bodies rushing all around him, the comedian rolled toward the yellow shirt's jittering body, plucking the blade free in one smooth motion. Foam escaped from the woman's mouth, and her eyes rolled back in her head as her heels pounded the pavement. Most of the wasters, upon seeing this, stopped in their tracks, thinking the comedian had hit her with some sort of magic. Their simple brains, never seeing

136

anyone die in such a manner, filled in the blanks, magic being the only explanation they could fathom.

"Him a wiz!" one of the wasters shouted.

"A wiggle-fingaz!" another shouted, and soon the wasters fled from the comedian, tumbling over each other to get away from the bemused man.

The comedian and Ajax stood panting, blood dripping down their faces. From above, one of the raftermen dove, his eyes locked on Side-Splitter. The comedian watched as this intrepid soul fell, his arms locked at his side, his head pointed at the concrete. At the last second, he spread his arms wide, using his open palms as wind resistance. He had only a split-second to wrap his hands around the hilt of Side-Splitter, a weapon which he thought to use against the comedian. But the funnyman wasn't having any of that. He dove at the man, bringing Rib-Tickler slicing across his forearms, opening two thin slices of red. The rafterman screamed, and the cord rebounded, sucking him into the air. At the end of his rope, literally, the rafterman jittered like a chicken with its head cut off. Blood and white flecks of foamy saliva spattered the ground.

The people in the rafters screamed their eagle screams, spat down at them, their fists pumping in the air, their mouths pulled into furious sneers to expose their yellow-brown, broken teeth.

As Ajax dropped the last of the yellow shirts to the ground with a concave forehead, the comedian turned and looked at her. "The natives are restless."

"Natives of what?" Ajax gasped, her chest heaving up and down.

"It's a saying."

"I don't get it."

"God, you're the worst. Let's go." The comedian sheathed his sword on his back. He didn't know what horrors awaited them on the Long Natural Path, but he would bet money Side-Splitter would be useless there. "Mind if I borrow this?" the comedian asked one of the dead yellow shirts. "Silence is acceptance," he said as he slid the strap of the shield over his forearm. When he turned, Ajax had liberated a shield as well.

"Is this Order?" the comedian asked her.

"It remains to be seen," Ajax replied.

"I kinda like it."

The serious look on Ajax's face didn't change at all, but he knew his answer bothered her.

Can't you just be nice for once? Oddrey asked.

The comedian didn't favor Oddrey with an answer. He merely stepped two steps to his right, jumped in the air and sliced the bungie cord of a diving rafterman. The cord broke with a loud snap, and the rafterman hit the ground with an even louder crunch, his arms breaking along with his neck.

"Clean up on aisle… uh… whatever the fuck aisle this is." The comedian laughed like a madman and then plunged down the Long Natural Path, Ajax following along, wondering what the hell she had gotten herself into.

Chapter 9: Uh...Maze-ing?

The quarters within the Long Natural Path were tight. On either side of Ajax, furniture rose to the ceiling, stacked in such a way that it was impossible to see through it. A feeling of claustrophobia settled in, and the air of the path was thick and heavy, the scent of the wasters who had passed through still hanging like a cloud between couches, beds, and bookcases.

The path was also gloomy, the only light being the reflection of strategically placed LEDs reflecting off the roof where the raftermen jumped and hooted. She didn't like it one bit. They moved slower now, the comedian's run slowing as soon as they stepped into the tight quarters.

All around them, Ajax felt eyes, and in the back of her mind she wondered if this was the way, if this was how she was meant to pave the broken road. It didn't feel right killing all these people, but somehow, she was able to make the situation fit within the twisted code of The Coop. *The regional manager broke a deal. Failed to keep his word.* That the comedian had forced the manager into doing this, with lies, was something she had yet to slot into the code. She didn't disagree with it, but the blood being spilled seemed unnecessary. There must be a better way.

Even as she thought this, a yellow shirt popped out of a large wardrobe, swinging his spiked shield at her. She bashed it to the side with her mace and drove her own shield into his throat, the tines plunging into the man's neck meat. When she pulled it free, rivers of red ran, and the man's hands went to his throat, his eyes wide. She hated it. Liked her mace better; it was less messy. A clonk on the side of the head usually put a person down fast, immediately. This poor waster had the time to think about death, to ponder what lay on the other side of this world. She hoped it was somewhere better, somewhere where the roads were still paved, and people didn't have to eat each other just to survive. She hoped, but didn't feel the hope, knew maybe this world was it. This was the one and only, the sole road of everywhere, so as the man gurgled and gagged, she apologized under her breath so the comedian wouldn't hear. If he heard, he would have something smart to say, and she didn't need that at the moment.

"Come on, Ajax. Plenty more where that came from."

Ajax turned and followed after the comedian. Elsewhere in Ike, the sounds of battle rang out, yellow shirts and wasters clashing as they tried to reach the regional manager. At the onset of the battle, Ajax had seen him turn heel and run. A coward, but a realistic one. The regional manager didn't seem to be the type of person who cleaned his own mess. His belly was round, not flat, and his arms were flabby. A sure sign of easy living. No one out in the wastes who carried their own weight had a body like that.

Ahead of them the path split as more raftermen dove at them, seeking to curry favor with the regional manager. After Ajax and the comedian side-stepped their attacks, the raftermen rebounded to the skies empty-handed. For a moment, she watched them do upside-down sit-ups, their abdominal muscles bunching as they grabbed the rope at their feet and began hauling themselves back into the rafters. Their athleticism and fearlessness spoke to Ajax. She admired them, didn't want to kill any of them. But sometimes, to pave the broken road, you had to kill the weeds sticking up through the cracks, and these people in the rafters were weeds for sure.

Onward they stalked, until the path split, heading off in two different directions.

"Well, do we stick together or split up?" the comedian asked.

"Not enough room to fight side by side in here," Ajax said, though she dreaded the thought of what the comedian would get up to left on his own.

"Right. If you see the regional manager, kill him. If you see Yokel or Beatums, free 'em up and bring 'em along."

"What if I find Cheatums?" Ajax asked.

"You leave him right where he is, bound and gagged preferably. He's a slippery one. You set him free, and you'll have a knife in your back before you can say poxyclypse."

Ajax nodded and took the left fork while the comedian took the right. After only a few steps, she could no longer hear him. "What have I gotten myself into?" she wondered aloud.

Onward she strode, her boots clomping on the concrete floor. It was impossible to sneak through the maze. She could have taken her boots off, tied them together by the shoestrings and hung them around her neck, but they could be a distraction, or worse yet, she could lose them altogether. She didn't know what would happen after this was all over, but she knew there would be plenty of walking; there always was. Boots were life in the wastes, or else you'd wind up like poor Vagsjon, with a hole in your foot and an inability to run from killer cats. The boots stayed on, which meant she was on high alert. She wouldn't be sneaking up on anyone.

That didn't bother her though. She much preferred it this way. *Let them know I'm coming. At least it's a fair fight then.* From above, she heard a rush of wind, and only had a split second to dive to the side as one of the raftermen plunged from the roof. The man swiped his arms at thin air and then rebounded into the sky.

From underneath a bed, a waster crawled. Once she found her feet, she leapt at Ajax with a length of metal gripped in her hand. Her blonde hair was so filthy it looked brown. She raised the metal bar into the air and swung it at Ajax. The Chicken Kicker, surprised by the woman's sudden appearance, took the blow in the chest. Much of its force was diffused by the chain mail she wore, but still it staggered her. The greasy-haired woman grunted like an animal and thought to press her advantage, driving Ajax backward and clawing at her eyes with her free hand.

Ajax brought her mace up underneath the woman's chin. Pain swirled in the woman's eyes as she spit teeth and blood in Ajax's face. Through her teary eyes, the woman backed away, growling. Then she looked up, and Ajax knew what came next. A great weight crashed into her. Spindly limbs wrapped around her body, and then she was sucked into the air, her legs flailing as her boots left the ground.

"I gotcher, girly," a dim voice said, and then she was being tossed through the air. Her head spun, and she felt nauseous as the world tilted around her, furniture, then wall, then rafters, then furniture some more. She was going to plummet to her doom, but before she did, another set of hands caught her. They were passing her like a game of stuffed rabbit from when she was a kid.

With her stomach reeling, she held onto her mace with a death grip, while she flailed about with the shopping cart shield secured to her wrist. Then she was spinning and tumbling again. This time she was prepared for it, and when the next rafterman came to catch her, she timed her attack just right, driving the pointed tines of the shield into the surprised man's face, while wrapping her arm around his now dead body. She dangled there, bouncing up and down, one arm gripping the stinking reek of flesh, held tight by the shopping cart shield buried in the man's face. He gurgled still, and Ajax chanced a look downward. It was a long way down, and even though she was only gently swaying, her head swam as if she was being passed through the air again.

Above, she heard scrambling, and in the shadows of the rafters, she spotted raftermen scrambling, knives in their hands. She was going to fall one way or another. Though it made her stomach roil, she scanned the floor below her. There, off to the right, she spied a mattress sandwiched between some bookcases, a stove, and some cabinets. *Lots of corners and edges down there.* But after looking down, she figured it would be better than the drop directly below. Beneath her, ten or twenty wasters waited, their faces upturned, their hideous teeth reflecting the diffused light of Ike.

They think they have me. Ajax smiled in the darkness, and began swaying the rope, lifting her legs and using her body as a fulcrum. The strength in her arms began to fail, and above, the rafterman had reached the spot where the bungie cord was tethered. *Only one shot, but such is life.*

Back and forth she swayed, swinging and pumping her legs, while the people below yelled intimidating threats at her.

"We's gonna nosh ya!"

"We's gon munch ya, girly!"

"Imma eat ya armpit!"

That last one was such a weirdly specific threat that Ajax couldn't help but look down to see who had said it. Before she could find them, the bungie cord broke free with a loud snap, and she went tumbling down to the ground. Spinning and falling, she sought to level herself out, but she was incapable of it. When she landed on the ground, it was a great surprise to her, as she landed on her back. From the impact of her body, wooden slats cracked, but then she realized she had landed exactly where she had expected—a cheap mattress dotted with multi-colored stains of the bodily fluid variety.

If anyone had been watching, they would have thought she had planned it. In reality, it had all been chance. She clambered down the treacherous pile of furniture, while the rafterpeople above screed like eagles.

"I want that pit!" Ajax heard a voice yell as she leaped from a dresser and landed back on the concrete once more. She ran then, willing the strength to return to her arms. Hanging for so long had sapped her strength, and she knew she would be sore tomorrow. She hoped the comedian was having better luck.

****

To the comedian, Ike was like a giant beast, and he was trapped in its insides, coursing through its intestines, lined with all sorts of furniture and bric-a-brac and other shit that no one needed. Had never needed in fact. A bunch of junk, piles of disposable crap. Think about all the work that had been done just to make that bookcase. The wood had to be cut, measured and milled. Metal had to be smelted, shaped into torturous hex bolts and finger-shredding Allen wrenches. Then another tree had to be cut down, treated with chemicals, bleached. Ink, stolen from the butts of squids, had to be collected.

What? Oddrey asked, incredulous.

"I don't know where ink comes from. But you get the point."

On your left.

The comedian brought up the shield, where it clanged against another shield, tines interlocking so he and a yellow shirt were stuck together, grunting and staring into each other's eyes. This one looked different from the others. He was tall, his face covered in yolking sores. The whites of his eyes were red, and his hands and arms shook. Other than the Lord of the Wrenches, he was the oldest living person he'd seen in Ike.

"An old-timer, eh." They circled around each other, their forearms locked together. "Not much time left by the look of those eyes."

"Aye, I'm old, so I am. But not too old to escort you to the exit."

"How long you been here?" the comedian asked.

"Since before the world ended."

"And you stuck around?"

"Hell, I like this place better now than I did before the world ended."

"Why's that?"

"The customers are a lot more polite when they know you can turn 'em into meatballs."

The comedian nodded his head. It was as good an answer as any. Then he plunged Rib-Tickler into the man's red eye. The man dropped to the ground, dead before he could even start shaking from the poison on the comedian's blade.

The comedian bent over to untangle the shopping cart shields bound to both their wrists. An eagle scree hit his ears, and he dove to the side, rolling onto his back. The rafterman left with empty arms. Above in the rafters, the comedian saw a dozen or so more, wrapping their tethers to the beams.

From deeper in the maze, more voices called out, violent voices.

"It's about to get bloody."

The comedian, a smile plastered to his face, readied himself, constantly glancing up to the sky and the industrious raftermen above. *Fucking bat motherfuckers.*

Around the corner came an onrush of yellow shirts, all older, skinny, and cantankerous as hell.

"We're gonna gut you, wasta!"

"Yeah, death for days, comin' your way, dusty boots!"

The comedian didn't bother replying. There was a time for humor and a time for survival. This was the time for killing.

Onward they came, their shopping cart shields clanking against ropes lined with Allen wrenches. Strange weapons, especially considering the narrow quarters in which they fought. To his left and right, stacks of furniture rose ten feet into the air, teetering precariously. Taking another glance at the rope in their hands, the comedian had a thought, and then, just as the thought crossed his mind, his prediction came true.

A man and a woman, taller and thicker than the others, stopped in the comedian's path, their shields held out to him, blocking off any attacks, the grids on their shopping carts shields too thin for his blade to penetrate. Behind the two who made a human wall, other yellow shirts uncoiled their ropes, flung them into the furniture on either side of the comedian and gave a mighty yank. The Allen wrenches threaded through the ropes caught on angles and knobs. When the yellow shirts gave a tug, the furniture came tumbling down, trapping the comedian underneath with his head and arms sticking out.

"Anyfing we can 'elp you with, wasta?" one of the men asked, his terrible wasteland accent ringing in the comedian's ears. He tried to move, to extricate himself out of the mess he'd gotten himself into, but he was trapped.

One of the men strode up to him, barefoot and stinking. He squatted down, his old man balls, popping out of his tattered khaki pants, covered in dark spots and lumps. "Any last words, funnyman?"

"Yeah. You oughta get those checked out. Testicular cancer is the number one killer of men your age, besides evercracks and raiders."

The old man looked down at his balls, a concerned look on his face.

146

"If you want, I can take care of 'em right now," the comedian said, wriggling the blade of Rib-Tickler around.

"Naw, I fink, I'll keep my bits for now."

Above, there was a commotion, and the comedian tried to crane his head upward to see what was happening, but he was unable. The scream was the first warning he had, followed by the splatter of a waster upon the ground. Another fell, and then another. It was raining wasters. Blood splashed the comedian's goggles, and the yellow shirt with the gnarly stones backed away, fear on his face.

"Whatsat?" he asked his companions.

"Looks like the cusses 'ave gotten into the beams."
More bodies fell down.

The gnarly-balled fella looked down at him. "See whatchu done, wasta? Ya gone and mucked it all up. Too many to eat now. Meat's gonna go rotten before we can process it."

A roar started behind the yellow shirts, and another gang of wasters came tearing ass through the maze. The confidence evaporated from the yellow shirts' face.

"Sounds like a lot of cusses," one said.

Gnarly balls looked down at him, and smiled. "Yer a lucky one, ain't ya?"

The comedian looked around at the pile of furniture trapping him and the dead bodies all around him. "Looks like it."

A dozen cusses, short for customers in the yellow shirts' parlance, skidded around the corner, their bare feet greasy and covered in blood. "Who ya fer, bruh?" the lead waster asked.

"We's fer corporate," gnarly balls answered. "Got da bossmang, right chere, ya know." Gnarly balls stepped out of the way, and the wasters craned their necks to see the comedian lying under the furniture.

"What's ma bruh doin' unna dere?" the waster asked.

"Uh… urm… quality control, me bruvs. Him's sussin' out da work we do."

"Well, let's get 'im up and get dat R.M."

Gnarly balls nodded, even as more bodies rained down from above. The lead waster giggled as a rafterman's body splattered to the concrete. "No more re-amazin' at nights, fam. How bow dat?"

"Good, good," gnarly balls confirmed.

The comedian, nothing more than a bit player in this game of cat and mouse, watched as the wasters began removing furniture, scaling the pile he was underneath as if it were a ladder. Behind them, he could see the yellow shirts conferring, and he knew what came next.

"Ere, bruh," the comedian said, speaking the waster language. "Dem yeller shirts ain't fer me. Deys fer the R.M."

"Wazzat?" the lead waster asked, clearly unable to grasp the comedian's attempt at the broken waster speech.

But it was too late. The yellow shirts, seeing the wasters occupied, swarmed over them, pulling them to the ground, and stabbing them in their important places with their shopping cart shields.

When they were finished, after almost no time at all, they looked down at the comedian, smiling.

"Where was we?" gnarly balls mused. "Right, carvin' you up."

"He's not yours to carve," a voice pronounced from above. The comedian couldn't see the speaker, but knew who it was from the austere, no-nonsense nature of the voice—Ajax.

Gnarly balls craned his neck upward, and his eyes went wide. Then he fell backward as Ajax leaped into view and clomped him on top of the head with her mace. His eyes rolled into the back of his head, and he fell backward. The other yellow shirts surrounded Ajax, but the quarters were tight, and only a few at a time could take their shot at her. The narrow confines gave Ajax the advantage, and their swings caught air or shield. The comedian was good, but Ajax was something else.

A whirling death machine, she spun and swung, lashing out with every part of her body, arms, legs, head. The initial wave of yellow shirts lay dying on the ground, and their compatriots stood casting questioning glances at each other. "Should we leave or should we die?" the looks seemed to ask.

Eventually, one man peeled away, and then another. Then the rest of the yellow shirts disappeared into the maze. The comedian lay with his lower body trapped, his head resting in his hands as if he was a child laying on the floor in front of a TV.

Ajax raised her hand in the air and flicked the blood and gore from her mace, splattering the concrete.

"I've saved your life again, Broken Man."

"Psshh. I had it all under control."

"Lies will be punished."

"Fine. Maybe I could have used the help, a little bit."

Ajax began pulling furniture off the comedian, and after a few minutes of tossing couches, tables, and bookcases, the comedian was able to extricate himself from the jumble of furniture.

"Well, we didn't split up for long, did we?" the comedian asked as another dislodged rafterman crashed down on the pile of furniture behind them.

The poor bastard groaned. "I can't move my legs!" he screamed. "Oh, they're going to ball me up for sure."

The comedian didn't care. He turned and headed deeper into the maze, Ajax following along, breathing heavy.

****

149

They wandered amongst piles of furniture, dead bodies and injured wasters everywhere. Some lay in heaps, their bodies punctured by lines of tiny holes from the yellow shirts' shields. Some lay twisted and beaten, stomped and kicked to death. The comedian might have felt something for them at one point, but right now, he was close to the end of his quest; he could feel it.

The excitement built and built until he could barely contain it any longer. For so long he had chased Cheatums, through town after town, ever since his first encounter with the man in a town far off, on the edge of the great salt waste, the part of the ocean floor that had been revealed after the ocean started to recede.

No one knew why the ocean had started to draw away from the coasts, but the comedian suspected the evercracks were not just a phenomenon particular to land. Somewhere in the ocean, he suspected you could find evercracks casting their witchy light into the sky while millions of gallons of water rushed into the holes, plummeting endlessly. It was a bad sign, a sign of the sure death of the planet, for without the oceans, they were screwed. How long would it take the world's oceans to drain? How long until the earth was a giant ball of dust with no water at all?

Certainly not before he could find Cheatums.

The gambler's face was faint in his mind. As he thought back, long and hard, digging through the mush of his brain without going back too far, to the damning times, he thought he could just recall Cheatums' almost attractive face.

****

Out among the sands, the bleached ribs of whales and dolphins jutted up out of the salty wastes. Fine, gritty grains of sand blasted across the one-time ocean floor. In the distance, the comedian could see the dark line of the ocean, receding like the gums of a man with scurvy. Once, before, this place had been a resort, the type of place people would visit on their vacations to sit, drink expensive wine, and stare out at the ocean. Far enough from any major cities, this town on the coast of what had once been California hadn't had to deal with typical things like fallout and mutated animals. Oh, they had their fair share of raiders and the occasional walking dead sighting, but the walking dead were easy to deal with.

Hell, the comedian wished the walking dead were his only problem. Contrary to popular horror tropes, zombies weren't all that big a deal. For one, they were slow as shit. For another, they weren't all that bright. They wandered the earth on their own, refusing to band together with others of their kind. They shuttled about the land as if the world revolved around them. Where you found one of the dead, seldom would you find another, for they were greedy and refused to share what was theirs. He supposed they were like billionaires in that way. Walking along, looking to ruin a random person's day, but also holding onto their spoils, fighting tooth and nail. Once, he'd seen a couple of the bastards duking it out over a corpse so old the skin was like tough leather. The battle had been slow and tedious, each of the zombies slowly squeezing the life out of the other and clawing the skin from each other's bodies. So interested had they been in their own petty world, they had completely ignored him as he strolled on by.

"Are you gonna make a move or what? Ain't got all day."

The voice belonged to a lanky man, needle-sharp nose that at first seemed charming, but now seemed long enough to find its way up your ass and ruin your day. Bright teeth, uneven, but clean, grinned back at him. Brown eyes, beady and shrewish, peered from a narrow face. The man was on the verge of being handsome, but the ever-

151

present sneer and air of superiority dashed all that in the comedian's eyes.

In his hand, the man fiddled with an ancient poker chip, twirling it across his knuckles. On the board between them sat pieces carved from seashells. It was a peculiar game, inherent to Carmel, which a third of the people pronounced as they had pre-war, a third pronounced it as Care-mel, and another third just called Caramel. Names changed. Better not to have one.

The man across from him, his lips pursed, chewed on the side of his mouth, his impatience showing.

The comedian looked down at the shells, carved into emoji shapes. He only barely understood the particulars of the game. Had lost quite handily at a warm-up round. On the wager table off to the side sat two treasures, the comedian's can of pork and beans and the gambler's can of Beefaroni, the type of cans that could keep a man alive for a week. Keep him bottom burping for a few days as well.

As the comedian pondered his next move—he really didn't know what he was doing—he reached out a hand and placed his fingers on an eggplant emoji. Faintly iridescent, it appeared to be carved from a muscle shell. Plenty of those out on the coast, out in the salty waste. As he touched his finger to the emoji, the man across from him tutted a bit, tsking his move.

But the comedian wouldn't be deterred. Not by a man named Cheatums. *Cheatums! The man, a gambler by trade, actually went by the name Cheatums!* He was either extremely overconfident in his abilities or completely idiotic. The comedian didn't know which.

As he was about to make his move, another man in the bar bumped into him, spilling his grog all over the comedian's jacket. The comedian should have known better than to react, to take his eyes off the board, but the thought of having to smell the stench of the swill they served in *The*

Pelican's Arse did not sit well with him. He stood and confronted the clumsy man, who immediately apologized and backed away, his hands in the air. When the comedian turned back, Cheatums sat with his arms crossed, pretending to study the board, but the comedian knew the board had changed, knew the pieces had been swapped around, though he had no proof.

"You cheated!" the comedian accused.

"How dare you?" Cheatums complained, genuinely sounding hurt.

"Your name is Cheatums! Of course, you're going to cheat."

"I would never." Cheatums looked around the bar and called out to all the salty sea dogs assembled in The Pelican's Arse. "Have any of you ever known me to cheat?"

"Naw, Cheatums cheat? Not on your life," said the man who had bumped into the comedian, a queer smile on his face.

The others in the bar shrugged and went back to their drinks. They didn't give a fuck, probably weren't on Cheatum's payroll like the clumsy gent with the too-clever smile he couldn't seem to wipe off his face.

"I declare shenanigans," the comedian announced, and immediately a gasp went up from the bar.

"Serious words, my friend. Serious words."

"I'm not your friend, and serious or not, I declare shenanigans anyway." There were few things that had spread throughout the wastes like the concept of shenanigans. A player, suspecting his competition was cheating, had the right to declare shenanigans at any time. The catch was, you had to put something up to pull it off, something of greater value than the initial wager, in this case a can of pork and beans and a can of beefaroni. But, if the accuser could cover the wager, then they could re-set the game, bring in a pair of impartial eyes who would get a cut of the wager. The comedian didn't need the extra set of eyes, but he did need a reset. Just looking at the board in front of him, he knew he was set up to lose, and he needed those beans and noodles.

"Well, what's your ante, and who's your eyes?"

The comedian fumbled in his backpack and pulled out a tin of sardines, ancient and tarnished.

Cheatums sat forward, his eyes gleaming. The Omega 3's in that tin were worth their weight in gold—you know, if gold still had any value. The salt, the fats, the proteins... definitely a match for a can of pork and beans.

"Sardines, eh." Cheatums sat back in his chair, pretending to mull it over. But the comedian knew he had him. Finally, after a great show of consideration, Cheatums nodded. "Alright. Deal. Now who's your eyes?"

The comedian could play too. He made a great show of scanning the room, pretending like he was weighing everyone in the bar. Cheatums probably thought he was going to pick one of the losers at the bar, their shoulders hunched over their beers. But instead, the comedian chose Cheatum's friend, the clumsy man with the too-obvious smile. Better to have him sitting at the table where he couldn't cause any damage or bump into him again. Cheatum's conspirator smiled even bigger now. No matter what happened, he would be getting a cut... a cut indeed.

Big Smile sat next to him, the boards creaking under his weight. He was a large fella, solid, probably used to throwing his weight around and getting whatever he wanted. But that wouldn't be happening today, not on the comedian's watch. He needed those beans, needed them to get the hell out of this place. He'd already done his show, received dick all for it on top of that. Carmel was a bust. If he was going to make it further up the coast, he would need nourishment. Oh, he could find stuff in the waste, wiggly plants to eat, rad-animals to munch on, maybe a scorpion or a brown widow to crunch between his teeth, get a little protein. But scouring the earth for bugs took time, and didn't offer much in the way of energy.

The comedian swiped the pieces off the board, swirled them around and dropped them into a bag. Watching Cheatums carefully, they alternated plucking pieces from the bag, building their armies. They placed them on the board, arranging and scattering their pieces on the chess board painted on a table that had once been a front door, but which now sat bolted to a couple of scavenged sawhorses. The goal of the game, much like chess, was to take the other person's pieces. The trick of the game was understanding how the pieces moved and which piece trumped the other. Each piece fell into one of three categories, much like rock, paper, scissors. Eggplant beat poop emoji, which beat beer emoji, which in turn beat eggplant emoji. None of it made much literal sense, and the comedian longed for a basic game of chess. Hell, even checkers would be better, but the old games dredged up old memories, which in kind brought up old traumas. So people invented new games, tested them out, saw what caught fire. Every town had its own games, often particular to their specific towns, hence emojis carved from seashells.

Carmel's population had been comprised of service industry professionals and celebrity survivors, who, in their general stupidity, had fled to the safest place they knew—a resort town on the edge of the coast. Not a lot of those celebrities were left. They weren't made to survive. Perhaps if they had developed their own shows, offered some form of entertainment to the people who did the everyday grinding and killing, they would have survived longer. But the majority of them were worthless. Without the benefit of social-media-likes and red-carpet premieres, their confidence flagged, and soon, when the sea began receding and the evercracks opened, people stopped caring about the movies they'd been in. The service population, realizing their new social standing after a few years, stopped kowtowing to the celebrities. The end result? A lot of familiar faces in the brothels and a lot more familiar faces rotting in the ground. Now, all the people left in Carmel were a hardy sort, the type who could work all day and drink all night.

"You gonna make yer move?" Cheatums asked. The comedian hated his voice. He talked in an exaggerated drawl like a movie cowboy. He thought this affectation made him sound cool, but it was so poorly done only an idiot couldn't see through it.

With a firm hand, the comedian slid a heart emoji out into the middle of the board, a three-by-three move with a hundred-percent emoji as backup. From there, the game was well and truly enjoined. Their hands flew across the board, sliding pieces this way and that. Each piece taken was a triumph. Each piece lost was a tragedy. On and on they went, Cheatums taking the early edge, but soon the comedian stormed back, swooping up eggplant, eyeball, and fire in three consecutive moves. Cheatums leaned forward and coughed into his hand, harder than he should have, and the comedian's concentration was broken. With Cheatums on the verge of losing, he was ready for the cheat.

As the comedian reached across the table, Big Smile, who had sat placidly the whole game, seeming not to care one jot about the outcome, bumped the table, sending the pieces sliding across the table.

"Shenanigans!" Cheatums announced loud enough for the whole bar to turn in their direction.

The comedian scoffed, "Shenanigans my ass! That's mutieshit and you know it!"

"Shenanigans, you cheating, vagabond bastard." Cheatums spat the words in his face, and the comedian felt the urge to unlimber Side-Splitter and chop the door and Cheatums in half. "You're in it with him!" Cheatums announced, pointing at Big Smile. The big man shook his

156

head, knowing if he admitted to cheating, he could be killed on the spot. It didn't matter that the comedian had never seen this man before. Didn't matter that they had never said more than two words to each other. In the eyes of the Carmel law, he either had to admit to cheating and fight for his life, or allow Cheatums a reset after he anted up once more.

The comedian, trapped in a pickle, waited for Cheatums to ante up.

"Well, let's see what you got."

Cheatums fumbled about his person, checking hidden pockets, reaching up his sleeves where the comedian saw a couple of dirty playing cards stashed for later. *Note to self: Don't play cards with Cheatums.*

The gamblers eyes went wide as he found what he was looking for. He pulled something shiny from a pocket and placed it on the pedestal next to the table. At first, the comedian dismissed the prize as nothing more than a trinket, and then he took one more look at the bauble, and that's when his rage consumed him. In the ensuing melee, a dozen Caramellers died, and Cheatums disappeared, fleeing through a bolt hole in the floor, its trick so cleverly concealed that by the time the comedian found the button to open the trapdoor, Cheatums was gone—long gone, the haul on the pedestal in his possession and an unstoppable enemy on his heels.

****

The memory faded, but his anger for Cheatums was kindled once more, just as fresh and raw as the as when he had first laid eyes upon that gleaming circle of pain. Back in the maze, he used his anger, perhaps his greatest gift, to drive him through its narrow, jumbled corridors. By now, word and whispers had spread about the comedian and his deadly fool, Ajax. Any people they saw fled from them, turning tail and running away.

"He's Def!" a yellow shirt yelled as he threw his shield to the ground and clambered up a pile of tchotchkes that went twenty feet high. It took a moment for the comedian to realize the woman hadn't been saying he was deaf, but that he was Death, the embodiment of the end. He smiled at the thought.

Eventually, after many twists and turns left the comedian's head reeling, they came to a door set in a wall, the maze continuing onward to their right. But the door interested the comedian. *This might be the regional manager's office.*

Without a word to Ajax, he lowered his shoulder and slammed through the door. It was unlocked and swung inward immediately, banging off the wall behind it. The comedian charged forward into a large room not unlike the warehouse in Alma. Racks, tall and empty, dominated the walls. All of Ike's goods had been assembled and put in the main part of the town. There were no empty boxes back here. Instead, the boxes had been flattened and spread out among the racks to create towering racks of bunkbeds.

Upon the comedian's entrance, the yellow shirts shrank against the walls of the warehouse space, eyeing the comedian with fear in their eyes. *It's Def,* they whispered amongst themselves. *And the fool.*

The comedian couldn't help but smile a bit at their nickname for Ajax.

"If yuz peepin' fer ya bunkboy, hims back dere wit da Lord," one fearful yellow shirt said.

"What the fuck did he just say?" the comedian asked Ajax.

"I think he said, 'Yokel's that way.'"

With a nod, the comedian strode past the yellow shirts who sat still as statues, their hands as far away from their shields as they could manage. If they didn't want a piece of *Def*, the comedian was happy to leave them alone. As he passed the sickly, cowardly employees of Ike he eyed them warily. Further on in the warehouse, they came to an office decorated with all sorts of Allen wrenches bent into strange, mystical symbols. The door to the office stood closed, but a closed door had never stopped the comedian. He was about to rear back and kick the door open when Ajax reached out and turned the knob.

"Try the handle next time."

The comedian shrugged. "You wanna get their filth on your hands, then by all means touch their germy doorknobs."

Ajax rolled her eyes, and they stepped inside to find Yokel bending the ear of Kallax.

"And then, Jeff says to Jesse Spano, 'You gonna win big in Vegas?' And Jesse Spano announced proudly, 'I'm gonna dance.'

"What the hell are you doin'?" the comedian asked Yokel.

"Oh, the Lord of the Wrenches, he wanted me to tell him his favorite movie. Look, he gave me my very own set of Allen wrenches in exchange. And I got your piano right here!"

The comedian, now that he stood before Yokel, was forced to admit he had been worried. But seeing him sitting here happy as a ghoul in a bomb crater transformed his worry into anger in a flash.

Aw, you really care about the little guy, Oddrey jibed.

The comedian conjured up all sorts of mean things to say, and then he turned, pushing Ajax out the door. "Stay here," he said over his shoulder before he slammed the door behind him.

"At least he's safe," Ajax said.

The comedian waved her comment away, and they returned to the maze to the whispers of "Def" and "fool."

159

Back in the maze it was quiet. The screams and the fighting had died down considerably, and the comedian wondered how many people were hidden away in secret compartments and hidden tunnels burrowing underneath mounds of furniture.

Onward they strode, twisting and winding through the shadowy innards of Ike.

"Maybe we should climb up on top of the furniture, like in Alma. Get the lay of the land."

It was a solid idea, one the comedian had entertained himself, but there was one problem. "I don't trust them. Suppose you get to the top and the furniture comes tumbling down. Could break a leg, or even worse."

Ajax nodded, so they pressed on through the maze. After what seemed like hours, the maze finally gave way opening up into… a cafeteria of all things. The lights in here were still functional through some miracle of wasteland engineering. The fluorescents overhead paled the companions' skin, made them look half dead, like a fresh member of the walking dead.

A gang of yellow shirts gathered around a shape crucified on the wall. As the comedian walked closer, the yellow shirts turned and smiled at him, their broken, rotten teeth reflecting the fluorescent light.

A woman, downright normal compared to the other freaks he'd seen in Ike, waved him on.

"We done as ye asked, strung 'im up right and propa, we did. Gave him the old pink slip."

The comedian studied the regional manager's face. His wrists and arms were affixed to a bed frame, Allen wrenches driven through his ankles and wrists. His head sagged, and he was clearly dead. The other… mutilations and adjustments they had made to the body were just cruel, and the comedian avoided looking at his tortured groin.

"Hims not Dinavian, so he's no good for meaty balls, but we can make do."

The comedian nodded at the woman.

Ajax stood with her mouth agape. The comedian reached out and pressed up on her chin, closing her mouth.

"Now, there is the matter of a couple of would-be employees, Beatums and Cheatums Sterling."

The woman nodded, smiling proudly at the work she'd done. "Follow me," she said, chipper and cheery. The companions followed. She strode across the cafeteria to a metal door. "When ya goes back to the head office, I hope ya tells 'em what I done. Yah?"

"You got it," the comedian said.

The woman pulled the metal freezer door open, and they stepped inside. On two metal tables, two men lay, eerily similar in aspect, though one was clearly more attractive than the other. Ropes and straps bound the men to the tables, their hands above their heads, their bodies naked. The man on the right was whole, but the man on the left had been… diminished somewhat.

"What did you do to them?" the comedian asked.

"What we's always done," the yellow shirt announced proudly. "When the old R.M. found out they was Dinavian, he had us drag 'em on the Long Natural Path. Meaty balls, my bossmang, it's what we's known fer. Sweedballs they used to call 'em I guess, back on the before tomorrow times. But, well, look around. We can't be choosers nor beggars in this dage. So, anything Dinavian'll go."

The comedian didn't understand a fucking word she said. "Piss off," he told the woman.

"Piss off what? A table?"

"Go away."

"Right. Youse da bossmang."

The yellow shirt turned and left them. The comedian placed a hand between the door and the frame, stopping the woman from sealing them inside. "Watch the door," he told Ajax.

She did as she was told, keeping one eye on the yellow shirts outside and one on the comedian inside. Her nerves were shot. Fighting through Ike had drained her, but the comedian didn't seem touched by all of the violence and carnage they had just wreaked upon the town of Ike.

Now that his quest was at an end, she was worried for him. Would completion of his quest pave the broken road or shatter it even further? She supposed she just had to wait and see.

****

The comedian walked between the two tables, examining the bodies laid out there. On the left lay Beatums, his eyes closed, his body naked. On the right rested his mirror image, or more aptly a funhouse mirror image. Anyone studying their two faces would see the familial connection.

It had been so long since he'd laid eyes upon Cheatums, so long since he'd been cheated out of the answers he wanted in Carmel. He could still see it, Cheatums' steady hand and nimble fingers reaching out to ante up a ring, golden, too small for most men's fingers back when he'd bought it, though the entire world was on a diet, so now it would be a fine ring for most people regardless of gender. He knew the ring, had designed it himself, drawn it up, taken it to the jeweler, and had it made.

The roping coils spiraling around its circumference, the thickness was just right, the etchings on the outside had been dulled by time and wear, but he still recognized it. It was his wife's ring.

Mom? Oddrey asked, her voice small and far away.

Back in Ike, the comedian broke out of his memories, rage appearing like a smothering cloud. He wanted to bash Cheatums to pieces, pull Side-Splitter free

162

and carve him into different cuts of meat and feed him to the people of Ike. The only thing stopping him was his need for information. He needed to know where Cheatums had gotten that ring.

Of course, Cheatums was in no mood to talk. The lower half of his leg was missing, a tourniquet tied tight around the upper thigh, a raw wound seeping onto the table.

He could kill him right now, but then he'd never know about his traitorous wife, if she lived or rotted in the ground somewhere. He prepared himself for the answers he would receive, knew he might not hear something he liked.

"Don't kill him," a voice said, melodious and smooth.

Beatums had awakened. The comedian spared him a glance, but otherwise ignored him.

"I'll play you for his life, just like back in Shithole. You name the game, I'll play."

"You got nothing I want. You're naked, and unless you've got a burrito shoved up your ass, I'm not interested."

With that, the comedian smacked Cheatums' face gently. His eyes snapped open, dirty brown things, beady and scanning the room for any sort of advantage. Then those eyes widened as they took in the face of his awakener.

"I knew you'd find me, sooner or later," he said, before breaking into a coughing fit. "Kinda wish you'd found me a little sooner," he said, glancing down at his missing leg.

"Oh, you wish I did, cuz then you'd be all two legged and running around doing your cheats and stealing wedding rings and running away and not telling people where you got the ring and all that shit." The comedian slammed his fist down on the metal table and Cheatums jumped, his beady eyes widening in fear.

"Don't, man. He's my brother," Beatums pleaded.

163

The comedian leaned in close, resisting the urge to take a bite out of the man's face. He wanted the man to suffer, even more than he already had. But still he needed the information. He stood and pulled himself away from the clean scent of Cheatums' skin. The comedian spun in a circle, his fists spasmodically opening and closing. In those hands, he imagined squeezing and twisting Cheatums' intestines.

Finally, his anger bottled up for the moment, he leaned over the suffering man, his hands firmly gripping the table. "You know what sucks, Cheatums? All I wanted to do was ask you a question, just one question. You could have had the beans, the ring, even the sardines; all I needed was information."

Somehow Cheatums managed to shrug on the table. "How was I to know? When a cheater cheats, it's best to make yourself scarce, and let's just say you don't read as the most sensible man. I was scared of you the moment I saw you." He coughed some more, and the comedian could see how pallid his complexion had grown. Cheatums wasn't long for the world.

"Tell me where you got it," the comedian said.

"I found the beans in an old retirement home, shoved under the bed of a—

"No, not the beans ya fuckin'—the ring. Where did you get the ring?"

"Oh yeah, the ring. Funny story. There I was in a game of skullcrack, and I was on a hot streak. I hadn't even had to wiggle my digits to keep ahead, if you know what I mean. That night I was hot, steamin' hot, like you could cook a rad-rabbit on my head if you needed to. I'm surprised the chair didn't catch on fire. I was so hot, there was a crowd around me, gathered around cheering me on as I spun the dice, cracking 'em off the kids' skulls. I was tearing it up man. I've never rolled the bones like that."

"Get to the point," the comedian demanded.

"Anyway, all of a sudden the crowd disappears. Vanishes like a flock of birds at a gunshot. They's just gone, and I'm sittin' there, like, well ok, guess I win the game. I'm scrapin' up my winnings and along come a lady, followed by two gnarly looking dudes who could break old Cheatums in two if they wished. So she sits at the table, and we get goin'. My hot streak continues, draggin' out like a hot summer night, and by the way her bodyguards are looking at me, I'm kinda wishing I *would* lose at some point."

"Wasn't long until she calls shenanigans, and for once, I ain't done shit. The bodyguards sit at the table, mean-muggin' me, and she throws this ring up there."

"What did she look like?" the comedian asked, leaning close to Cheatums, His words had started out strong, but they were fading.

Cheatums stretched his neck out, trying to focus on the comedian's face. "She was mean looking. Like the bodyguards were one thing, but they were just big muscle toughs, freaks. But the look on her face, I ain't never seen nothing like that. Kinda reminded me of you actually. Tattoos on her face, tribal, post-death style tats. Folks called her Mama Turner. She was big weight out there."

"Out where?"

Cheatums' eyes rolled into the back of his head, and the comedian slapped him gently on the face, trying to get him to hold on for a bit longer. "Out where, motherfucker?"

"Leave him alone," Beatums complained. "Let him rest."

But the comedian hadn't come this far just to let the answers he sought fade away in death. Slap. Slap. Slap.

As Cheatums groaned, his eyes rolled back to their proper places in his sockets. "Where did you meet Mama Turner?"

Confused, Cheatums groaned, "Mama Turner?"

165

"With the ring, the bodyguards, Mama fuckin' Turner."

Cheatums' Adam's apple bobbed up and down, and he choked the words out. The comedian backed away from him, his hands falling to his side.

"Are you done now? Did you get what you wanted?" Beatums shouted. "Cut me loose."

But the comedian didn't hear the pleas of the gambler. He was too busy digesting the words of Cheatums. *"Fortress"... impenetrable, armed, populated by the deadliest gang of control lords in the history of the wastes. "Of"... a preposition, uhh... what the fuck is the definition of "of"? "Good"... supposedly something positive, something that makes lives better. Put it all together and what do you have? The motherfucking Fortress of Good.*

The comedian strode past Ajax, who stood studying him. He had no time for her and her preaching. There was a long way to go yet. The wheels in his head started turning, dust falling from the gears and rust flakes chipping away as those dormant gears began to turn once more.

Ajax watched him go.

"Ere now," one of the yellow shirts called. "Which of us has been promoted to regional manager, bruh?"

The comedian strode past, pointing a finger at the woman he'd told to piss off. In Ike it was quiet, but for the frantic speaking of one man to his dying brother.

Chapter 10: Brothers

The dangerous woman untied Beatums, and it took him several minutes to get the circulation back into his extremities. In the meantime, he flailed about on the metal table, trying to sit up with two arms that had succumbed to pins and needles. It was like trying to push yourself up with a set of noodles attached to your shoulders.

Tears filled Beatums' eyes as he soaked in the poor state of his brother. His brother was manipulative and a crook, but at least he never lied about who he was. Right then and there, Cheatums was the only thing remaining of Beatums' past, the only sign in this world he would be remembered. His brother, who until he was seventeen, had always had his back. In this world, that meant something.

Of course, then Cheatums had discovered beer, women, and gambling, and his regard for Beatums had gone right out the window. And who could blame him? It was a shit world, and there were only a few good things left in it. The love of a brother was one of those things, and while his brother had been distant and more of a pain in the ass than he ever would have expected when they were growing up, the prospect of losing him was untenable.

Beatums fell from the table, his feet and legs still asleep. On his knees, he threw his noodle arms up onto Cheatums' table, and somehow managed to pull himself to his feet. The skin of his wrists and ankles still showed the red and purple marks of ropes. With his dead hand, he slapped his brother in the face. His eyes fluttered open and it took an agonizing time for those eyes to focus on Beatums' face.

"Hey, brother."

"Hey," Cheatums answered back.

"You need anything?"

"Just sleep."

Beatums nodded. When he blinked, his tears splattered and spread in his eyelashes, hanging there. Beatums had never seen his brother like this. He'd seen him take beatings that would have killed another man. And yet, the next day he'd be out there with broken ribs and black eyes trying to earn whatever the hell he could to keep himself, and sometimes his younger brother, fed.

Life had been hard for them, growing up under the uncaring eye of a man who had gifted his children with absolutely stupid fucking names. But together, they had been an unstoppable force, had grown into their names. Beatums was well aware everything he'd learned about gambling had been taught to him by his piece of shit brother. By the look of his brother's face, and the lines running up his leg, dark and ominous, death would be his brother's final lesson.

"Beatums?" Cheatums asked, his eyes searching for his face though it was right in front of him.

"I'm here, bro." Beatums grasped Cheatums' hand, squeezed it, and his brother squeezed back, ever so lightly.

"I don't want you to end up like me. Don't do it."

"What are you talking about? You're awesome."

Tears gathered at the corners of Cheatums' unseeing eyes. "No. I mean it. I know you've always looked up to me, and I should've been more responsible about it. Truth was, I knew I was a piece of shit from the day I was born. You looking up to me… it was the only thing I ever had."

Beatums' lower lip began to tremble.

"I should have done better than what I did. I should have taught you to do something else. Don't be like me. Don't gamble anymore. It's no way to live. You're better than that, better than me, always have been."

"Shut up," Beatums slurred, his chin trembling.

"Listen. Listen. Don't cry, bro. Don't cry. I'm gonna tell you something, and I want you to do with it what you

168

will. You was always smart like that. You hear me? Beatums?"

"I hear you," Beatums stammered.

"I want you to stop gambling. Nothing good ever came of it. You ever seen an old gambler in the waste?"

Beatums shook his head. He was having trouble speaking.

"Beatums?" Cheatums called, his head moving side to side as if searching.

"No. No old gamblers. None."

"I want that for you, brother. I want you to get old. Live life, remember me, but don't be me. Can you do that?"

"I can do that."

"Good. Now kill me."

Tears fell from Beatums' eyes, and his voice remained locked in his throat.

"I'm done man. You can't stay here, and as soon as you leave, they're gonna eat on me. I know that's my fate. All that cheating led me here. So, you gotta do what you gotta do, bro."

Logically, he knew it was the best solution, but he wasn't ready for it. A ragged sob escaped his throat.

"None o' that now. It ain't no big deal. I had a good run, but when the emojis don't line up, they don't line up. I done cheated my way out of everything, but you can't cheat Mr. Rot. He's gonna come for you sooner or later, and he knows all the tricks. Plays 'em himself all the time."

"I can't," Beatums moaned.

Cheatums smiled, nodding. "I know. It ain't in your nature. You were always the good one. Send in one of them people then, the ones what saved us."

Beatums leaned forward and gave his brother a hug. Cheatums, using the last of his strength, returned the embrace. They sat that way for a long time, remembering the days of their youth, spent in an old junkyard with their old man, their mom long dead in a raider attack. Dad had

169

been rough with them, manning them up too soon. But through it all, they had each other. On their own, they would have died. They'd pulled each other out of the fire more times than they'd care to admit.

Sniffling Cheatums said, "Go on now. This place is bad, and I'd just as soon get onto the next one."

Beatums stepped into the cafeteria, calling over the Chicken Kicker whose name he didn't quite remember. She stepped to him with a curious look on her face, her hand resting on the gnarly mace hanging from her belt.

"I need to ask you a favor."

No response, just that curious look.

"I need you to give him the Kiss of Mercy."

The curious look faded away, replaced by the soft eyes of sympathy. She touched his shoulder once. He took a deep breath and swiped the tears off his cheeks. Together they stepped into the freezer. When Ajax dragged the blade, Beatums averted his eyes, though he did manage to hold onto his brother's hand until his last breath.

Chapter 11: The Companionship

The companions gathered in the Lord of the Wrenches' room, yellow shirts and wasters alike parting for them. They stood with proud faces. "Unionized" was the word that went around the room when they talked about the slaughter, as in "We just unionized real good." The word's connotation had undergone something of a transformation. Instead of meaning "the process to form a labor union," unionized, in this context, meant clearing away all the cracks and divisions between the people of Ike. They were one now, though how long that would remain was anyone's guess.

The comedian didn't think it would take that long for them to break down. It's not like any of them were rocket scientists, and their reliance on cannibalism and raiding Alma as a source of food spelled disaster down the road. Only so much long pig a body could eat before they twisted and got sick, as evidenced by shaking hands and a diminished mental capacity. Once the leaders got the shakes, the town could wind up anywhere. But it wasn't the comedian's problem. Nothing in the wastes was, except for one thing—finding the owner of the ring.

The Lord of the Wrenches, Kallax, sat on his knees, his collection of wrenches laid out before them.

In one smooth motion, he swooped the Allen wrenches up and dashed them against the concrete floor, where a few made sparks. He leaned forward, his bulbous nose protruding from the edge of his robe's hood, studying the wrenches and trying to make sense of them. The comedian put no stock in Kallax's reading, but it was always good to leave on a high note. Sometimes, the people of a town made up stories about the visitors who came to their settlement, made them out to be more than they were, and when it was time to leave, sensing a greatness in you they themselves had manufactured, they would gift you things. This was part of the process, and they had done much for Ike, "unionizing" it and mending the rifts in the community.

Finally, Kallax reared up, his head thrown back and his arms spread wide. Once again, the comedian admired his showmanship, took a few notes. If he could find a reliable fortune teller, those notes would come in handy.

As Kallax spoke his words, they went in and out of one ear. The comedian was too busy standing stunned at his own thoughts. *Find a fortune teller?* He scanned the people standing around him. Ajax stood off to his left, her legs spread and her hands held behind her back, lapping up every word from the Lord of the Wrenches' mouth. Yokel sat on the ground to his right, his jaw agape as he devoured Kallax's every word, boyish simplicity on his face, like a kid seeing their new favorite movie for the first time. Apart from their group stood Beatums Sterling, his shoulders shrunken with grief. In a locker they'd found his gear, and he stood once more in a fur-lined denim vest, a green gambler's visor perched jauntily on his head. The comedian didn't know where Beatums fit in, but he could feel it, feel that he was a part of this.

Don't forget me, Oddrey added.

How could I ever forget you, Oddrey?

Eventually, Kallax's predictions and prognostications, couched in double-talk that could mean anything, wound down, and he focused his eyes on the four—

You forgot about me! Oddrey shrieked.

—five individuals standing in front of him. In rich, old man tones, Kallax spoke to the comedian, "It is an odious task, but I sense much riding on it. This ring you have seen, you must find its owner and settle your soul. For in doing this, you settle the souls of us all, and halt the rot of the world, which has died and breathed its last breath.

But go alone, and you shall fail. This task is too great for one such as yourself, mighty though you be."

"You shall have my mace at your side," Ajax declared.

"And my twisted metal scrap," Yokel chimed in.

Then surprisingly, out of nowhere, Beatums, who had just lost his brother, chimed in. "And you'll have my… uh, charm, I guess. I don't really use weapons."

The words had a faint, familiarity to them that the comedian could not place.

"Go then to the Fortress of Good and seek ye the owner of this ring, for in so doing, the world shall be changed, and all shall be turned right once more. I dub thee the Companionship of the Ring."

"Surely there are some copyright issues with all of this," the comedian said. The others just scratched their heads, having no clue what the comedian was talking about. For his part, the comedian found he didn't mind the company, looked forward to it in fact. Though Beatums bore watching. He doubted Beatums' sincerity, thought maybe he would stab him in the guts in the middle of the night for the role he had played in Cheatums' downfall.

"High five," the comedian said to the Lord of the Wrenches. Kallax put his gnarled paw in the air, and the comedian slapped his shaking palm, the sound ringing out amongst the Ikeans. With that done, the comedian looked around the room and asked, "Y'all got anything to eat that wasn't people?"

The Ikeans laughed at his joke, and the Companionship of the Ring went hungry that night.

Chapter 12: Campin'

A fire burned bright but low under the radglow, outlining the wasters in green light. From the corner of his eye, the comedian could see Beatums' boot tips pointed up at the sky. He never let Beatums out of sight, didn't trust him at all. Any day now, he expected the man to make an attempt on his life.

Across the fire, Yokel lay on his side, his head propped up on one elbow, staring into the coals, probably imagining old movies, replaying them in his radiator-fluid damaged brain.

To his right, Ajax juggled the comedian's balls, sending them into the air, one by one, her hands whirling so fast he could barely keep track of them. He'd taught her a few lessons that night. She was a quick study, but still, nowhere near what she would have to be to pull a round of applause and some swag from an audience. But practice made perfect, and between here and the road to the Fortress of Good, there was plenty of time for that.

The comedian knew of the Fortress of Good, had heard tales of it in his travels for years. Originally a theme park, the new inhabitants, raiders and wasters, had taken over the place, establishing a hideout that had become a settlement and then a city. There were few places in the wastes able to claim the status of city, but the Fortress was one of them. Deep to the south, in the mountains nearest the west coast, the Fortress of Good jutted up into the sky, sending a light into the air as a beacon, calling wasters, gamblers, and raiders alike, a desert siren with a nice rack and pointed, carnivorous teeth.

With their newfound population, the city had become more... civilized. Nothing compared to what towns were like before the death of the world, but close. If you knew the rules and the laws, you could live there, stay alive. But if you broke the rules, punishment was swift and severe, which was why the story of the Fortress of Good had spread so far and so wide in such a small amount of time. There were always those looking to escape the reach of the fortress, people who had crossed the law and were now slated for the gleaming gibbets of the Fortress' walls.

In that Fortress existed someone who had once held the wedding ring he had designed for his wife. Mama Turner they called her. Whether this person was, in fact, his wife, or just someone who had killed his wife and taken her ring, or any of another hundred possibilities, remained to be seen, but he was going to find out. Between here and the Fortress lay a thousand miles. A thousand miles of wasteland, strange settlements populated by cannibals, surreal new societies, and the occasional band of the walking dead, amongst other, more exotic monstrosities.

The weight of that journey pressed down upon him, made him lean back into the burnt soil.

Did the ring belong to Mama? Oddrey asked.

The comedian grumbled his assent.

What if Mama Turner is actually Mama?

"I don't know."

The sound of Ajax dropping his balls offered him no amusement. He wasn't feeling all that funny today.

Are you going to kill her?

"Maybe."

Oddrey went silent, and though he didn't want to relive his past, the possibility that this Mama Turner was his wife kept him up all night. When Beatums rose to hover over the comedian in the middle of the night, he didn't even open his eyes, just waited to hear the unsheathing of a knife and the split of his skin. Eventually Beatums went away, and soon he could hear the soft snorings of his ragtag group of performers.

When the waste sun rose, burning his skin with its horrific, pumpkin-colored light, he sat up, groaning and staring at the blowing ash of the dead fire. A wind rose from the north, cold and laced with the smells of far-off rot. It blew against his back, and he stared off to the south, trying to see through the miles and miles of mountains and waste between him and the Fortress of Good. *Are ya there, my wife? I'm coming for you if you are.*

When the others awoke, they kicked dirt over their campfire, shouldered their packs and gear and set off in the direction of the comedian's choosing, their boots kicking up dust, their breaths singing in their lungs. It was a long road to the Fortress of Good, and there was a lot of bad between here and there, but at least he had the brick of silver snuggled away in his pack for the long road ahead..

Step by step, they began their journey, the threads of their lives intertwining to form a thin rope, just strong enough to hang themselves with.

A Word From Jacy

Thank you for reading *One Night Stand in Ike*! I hope you've been enjoying the comedian's crazy adventures. If you have, please leave a review! As an indie author, the only marketing I receive is from fellow readers like you!

If you enjoyed One Night Stand in Ike, check out the fourth book, One Night Stand in a Place with No Name! The comedian's journey continues! Laugh along with the comedian as he encounters a strange group of people in a bomb shelter as he continues his journey to the Fortress of Good. Right now, I'm not sure how many books will be in the series, but if it goes on forever, I wouldn't mind, as I have so much fun writing them! In the meantime, I'll be working on the next installment!

One Night Stand in a Place with No Name will be available on amazon soon!

Get Free Stuff from Jacy Morris

Building a relationship with my readers is super important to me. Please join my newsletter for information on new books and deals plus all this free content:

1. A free copy of This Rotten World: Part One.

2. A free copy of The Lady That Stayed, a horror novella inspired by real life.

3. A free copy of The Pied Piper of Hamelin, a twisted fairy tale like nothing you've ever seen before.

You can get your content for free, by signing up at https://landingpage.jacymorris.com/home-copy-1

Also By Jacy Morris

In the One Night Stand Series

One Night Stand at the End of the World

The world is gone, and it's not coming back. The rules have changed, but one man refuses to lay down and die. A comedian, shattered and broken, wanders the wasteland on a quest that only he knows and understands. Zombies, raiders, talking doll heads, shady merchants and unbeatable gamblers all stand in the way of The Comedian's success, but through the power of comedy, he will find a way.

Available on amazon!

One Night Stand in the Wastes

Book two in the One Night Stand series. With his sights set on a mysterious place named Ike, the comedian journeys across a shattered and broken wasteland, confronting demons both inner and outer. Behind him, justice dogs his footsteps in the form of Ajax, a ruthless arbiter of order who is hellbent on ending the comedian's chaotic ways. Killer squirrels, mutated humans, and raiders galore await the comedian in the blasted lands.

Available on amazon!

One Night Stand in Ike

Book three in the One Night Stand series. After journeying across the wastes, the comedian and his companion finally make their way to the town of Ike. There they find a twisted world based upon the rules of corporate society. In order for the comedian to complete his quest, the pair of survivors must play by the rules of Ike's regional manager… or they could, you know, kill everyone. We'll see.

Available on amazon!

One Night Stand in a Place with No Name

Book Four: The comedian and his gang of entertainers head toward the Fortress of Good in the hopes of finishing his mission. Of course, travel in the wasteland isn't as easy as it used to be, and they are waylaid in a mysterious town.

Coming Soon!

In the This Rotten World Series

This Rotten World

A sickness runs rampant through the world. In Portland, Oregon it is no different. As the night takes hold, eight men and women bear witness to the horror of a zombie outbreak. This Rotten World is the zombie novel that horror fans have been waiting for. Where other zombie works skip over the best part of a zombie outbreak, This Rotten World revels in it the downfall of humanity, dragging you through the beginnings of society's death, kicking and screaming.

Available on amazon!

This Rotten World: Let It Burn

It didn't take long for Portland, Oregon to fall. Amid a decaying and crumbling city, a group of survivors hides amid the smoke and the fire. They need to get out of the city... which is easier said than done with thousands of zombies blocking the path. Witness the terrifying flight of these survivors as they leave the city behind and Let It Burn.

Available on amazon!

This Rotten World: No More Heroes

With the smoking ruins of Portland behind them, our survivors find that they have a new enemy to contend with... other survivors. With the dead hounding them at every step and humanity struggling to hold onto its civility, the survivors face their greatest challenge yet. At the end of this battle, there will be No More Heroes.

Available on amazon!

This Rotten World: Winter of Blood

Winter falls hard on Oregon, burying the world under snow and ice. One group of survivors, stuck in a tomb of their own creation, fights to survive, while another group treks across the snowbound countryside, leaving a trail of bloody footprints in their wake… and an army of the undead. The Pacific Ocean calls. Safety calls. But as Mother Nature rakes her frozen claws across the land, the coast could hardly seem further away. Will our survivors make it through this Winter of Blood, or will they be buried by an avalanche of the dead? Find out in the thrilling 4th installment of This Rotten World... This Rotten World: Winter of Blood.

Available on amazon!

This Rotten World: Choking on the Ashes

As our survivors near the coast, the road takes its toll. Falling apart physically and emotionally, they are drawn to the siren call of the beach. Seaside awaits them, a town demolished by a tsunami and crawling with the reanimated. With infants in tow, the survivors must band together to fight for a new home. All that stands between them and the future is an army of the dead. Will they succeed, or will they find themselves Choking on the Ashes?

Available on amazon!

This Rotten World: Rally and Rot

Introducing an entirely new cast of characters, Rally and Rot continues This Rotten World's tradition of zombie excellence. Every summer, Monktree, Wyoming holds a biker rally, an underground event policed by the bikers themselves. When a tragic accident kicks off the zombie apocalypse, the survivors must band together to make it out of town.

Available on amazon!

In the Enemies of Our Ancestors Series

The Enemies of Our Ancestors

In the mountains of the Southwest, in the time before the continents were known, the future of the entire world rested upon the shoulders of a boy prophet whose abduction would threaten to break the world. As a youth, Kochen witnessed the death of his father at the hands of a gruesome spirit that stalked his village's farmlands. From that moment forth, he became a ward of the priests of the village in the cliffs. As he grew, he would begin to experience horrific visions, gifts from the spirits, that all of the other priests dismissed. When the ancient enemies of the Cliff People raid the village and steal Kochen away, they set in motion world-changing events, which threaten to break the shackles that bind the spirits to the earth. A group of hunters are sent to bring Kochen back to his rightful place. As Kochen's power grows, so too does the power of the spirits, and with the help of an ancient seer and his hunter allies, he seeks to restore balance to the world as it falls into brutal madness.

Available on amazon!

The Enemies of Our Ancestors: The Cult of the Skull

With the world balanced after the tragedies of the year before, two tribes attempt to come together and form a whole. But as an ancient foe from the past reappears and a new threat from the south snakes its way to them, the Stick People and the Cliff People must do more than put their differences aside... they must come together to survive. As fantastic as it is violent, The Cult of the Skull picks up right where The Enemies of Our Ancestors left off.

Available on amazon!

The Enemies of Our Ancestors: Broken Spirits

Time has passed. The children of the tribes have grown. Peace has reigned as three tribes have tried to learn to live together. But now, an old terror rears its head. Together, the three tribes will have to learn to fight as one. The thrilling conclusion to The Enemies of Our Ancestors series.

Available on amazon!

Standalone Novels

The Abbey

In the desolate mountains of Scotland, there is an abbey that time has forgotten. Its buildings have crumbled, and the monks that once lived there, guarding the abbey's secret, are long dead. When the journal of a crazed monk is discovered, so is the secret of Inchorgrath Abbey. There are tunnels underneath the abbey and in them resides a secret long forgotten. Together with a group of mercenaries, her would-be boyfriend, and her cutthroat professor, Lasha Arkeketa will travel across the world to uncover the secret of The Abbey.

Available on amazon!

The Drop

How many hearts can a song touch? How many ears can it reach? How many people can it kill? When popular boy band Whoa-Town releases their latest album, no one thinks anything of it. They certainly don't think that the world will be changed forever. After an apocalyptic disease sweeps the world, it becomes clear that the music of this seemingly innocuous boy band had something to do with it, but how? Katherine Maddox, her life irrevocably changed by a disease dubbed The Drop, sets out to find out how and why, to prevent something like The Drop from ever happening again.

Available on amazon!

The Pied Piper of Hamelin

A sickness has come to the village of Hamelin. Born on the backs of rats, a plague begins to spread. As the town rips itself apart, a stranger appears to offer them salvation. But when the citizens of the town fail to hold up their end of the bargain, the stranger returns and exacts a toll that is still spoken of to this day. That toll? The town's entire population of children. This is the legend of the Pied Piper. It is no fairy tale. It is a nightmare. Are you prepared to hear his song?

Available on amazon!

Killing the Cult

At any one time, there are 4,000 cults operating within the United States. In Logansport, Indiana, one cult is growing. When The Benevolent recruit Matt Rust's estranged daughter, he journeys to their compound to free her, one way or another. Unfortunately, for Matt Rust, his checkered past threatens to derail his rescue mission. When word gets out that Rust has reemerged after spending the last decade in the witness protection program, drug tzar Emilio Cartagena sends his best men after Rust. Will he be able to save his daughter before Cartagena's men arrive? Find out as Matt Rust tries Killing the Cult.

Available on amazon!

The Lady That Stayed

Land has a price. It's always been that way. When J.S. Stensrud and his wife Dotty buy a piece of land on the Oregon coast known as the Spit, they come to know that price. As Stensrud tries to build a legacy on his island amid the background of the Great Depression, he is visited by a Native American woman who helps him learn the bloody price of land in the most painful way possible.

Available on amazon!

The Taxidermied Man

Bud got stuffed, and now he has a front row seat to the downfall of man.

Suffering from early-onset dementia due to alcoholism, Bud wants nothing more than to be there for his wife forever—so he has his body stuffed. Unfortunately, his wife is not at all pleased, and after she dies, Bud is sold off to the highest bidder only to be used as a sex toy, a sports trophy, and finally a God. As his imprisoned mind unravels, Bud witnesses the collapse of humanity through static eyes and an unchanging body.

Available on amazon!

An Unorthodox Cure

Cancer will touch all of our lives at one point or another. It may affect someone you know, someone you respect, or even someone you love. In the case of the Cutters, it has systematically invaded every cell of their daughter's body. When the doctors admit there is nothing they can do, the Cutters bring their daughter home and prepare to wait for the inevitable. Just as they accept defeat, a mysterious doctor appears at their door, offering a miraculous cure and kindling hope in their hearts. The only catch? The Cutters have to decide what is more important, their daughter's life or her soul.

Available on amazon!

About the Author

Jacy Morris is a Native American author who has brought to life zombies, cults, demons, killer boy bands, and spirits. You can learn more about him at the following:

Website: http://jacymorris.com

Email: jacy@jacymorris.com

Facebook:
https://www.facebook.com/JacyMorrisAuthor/

Twitter: https://twitter.com/Vocabulariast

Be sure to check out

THE

DROP

By Jacy Morris

Here is a sneak preview:

PROLOGUE

An excerpt from an article entitled "Whoa-Town Becoming Whoa-World in Record Time" by Anton Russo as Published in *Rolling Stone*

Part of me wants to hate them. Boy bands aren't supposed to be this good. A man, a grown-ass, thirty-year-old man, shouldn't find himself moved by the vocal-stylings of five boys, some not even old enough to drink yet. But here I am, at Wembley Stadium, packed in like cattle in a slaughterhouse chute, ready to stick my head into the kill box and have a hole punched in my cranium.

There is no opening band for Whoa-Town. What sucker would take that gig? Who would want to have the memory of their performance obliterated by the next act, a band that many claim is bigger than the Beatles and the Stones combined? Lofty words. All of us scoffing, bearded, music snobs sneer, knowing full well in our hearts that there is no way anyone means it when they throw out those comparisons. It's just the thing that clichéd, hack journalists say when they can't think of any way of telling people how big a band is or is going to be.

Here I am, standing amid the heat and the hot breath of 90,000 people, the lucky ones who snagged their tickets in that first two minutes before the entire system crashed. Leading to a day in London collectively known as Cry Day, the day that every teenage girl, and many other men, women, and boys christened their cell phones with tears at news that the Whoa-Town show was already sold out.

You'd expect the air to reek of cheap designer-knockoff perfume, hair product and bubblegum. But it doesn't. It smells of something else. It reeks instead of lust and anticipation. The crowd hums with energy; their faces drip sweat even though the stadium's roof is open to the elements. The cool night air can't compete with their fever. Their bodies vibrate, conducting heat at a level that confirms in my mind that spontaneous combustion might actually be a thing. At any moment, the girl next to me, screaming ear-piercing "woos" every thirty seconds or so, might burst into flames.

Before long, we can't take it anymore. Wait... they can't take it. I'm certainly not into any boy band. I'm just here for the story. They begin to chant. When the mother next to me, clad in baggy jeans that go up past her bellybutton, elbows me as encouragement, I make a show of reluctantly joining in. I clap. I yell, "Whoa-Town!" right along with everyone else.

Only when the building quakes from all the stomping, yelling, and clapping does something happen. Just as I am assured that Wembley Stadium will collapse around us before the band ever takes stage, the lights come on, blinding us. The lights fade, dropping faster than my own aloof persona, plunging us into a darkness punctuated by the unwelcome glow of emergency lighting. Around the stadium, tiny rectangular blooms of blue-light illuminate in response. 90,000 people recording when they aren't supposed to be. It is as if the stadium is filled with thousands of mutant fireflies, swaying from side to side as the chant of "Whoa-Town!" thunders through the stadium once again... and then the beat drops.

With a "whoomp," several sparking shapes arc into the air, erupting into gold and crimson starbursts, and screams echo so loudly that I'm not even sure when the screaming stops and the music begins. They're here. Whoa-Town, the boys that will change music and the world forever and I, Anton Russo, was there.

Tragic. Just tragic. - Sebastian

You think that's tragic, check out those *Teen Beat* articles I found. - Katherine

Chapter 1: Walking the Streets

I see this story as more than a job, more than just a fact-finding mission to once again help us cope with the tragedy, with a loss that, in a very real sense, is unprecedented. Many people have tried that. So many. No, if that's all this was, then I would be off somewhere else, looking into a murder or trying to uncover the next dastardly person exploiting the American Relief Organization.

I see this story as a time capsule, a way to help the people of the future. If there's one thing that I learned from my 8th-grade social studies teacher, it's that history is a cycle, and that all things, good or bad, will come around again, hence the term revolution, a circuit, a never-ending loop that only the educated can see. Thinking about what the world has just gone through, and is still going through, I can only shudder at the thought that hundreds of years down the line this will all happen again. So my hope is to write this story, bury it in the ground, and when it's needed, the people of the future can come and dig it up.

People will need to know, not so much the people that are still alive, but the people of the future. The people still alive already know about The Drop. They're so tired of thinking about it that they don't actually want to know the truth of the situation. They can't help but see The Drop around them. Examining it further is just poking at a poorly stitched together wound with a razorblade. Sooner or later it's going to open up. Sooner or later, it's going to bleed. They don't want to know how the knife that stabbed them in the chest was forged. They don't want to know where the steel came from, how the ivory handle was carved from the tusk of a poached elephant. None of that will help them. But for the people of the future, that's a different story altogether. The Drop was our Black Plague, and just as our knowledge of the spread of the plague prevents it from happening again, this article is vital to preventing another Drop.

I'm in the Big Apple. They call it the Big Rotten Core now. As I walk down Broadway, I'm struck by its similarity to the post-apocalyptic movies I over-consumed as a teenager. The emptiness of the streets, very *I Am Legend.* The newspaper tumbling through the intersection, unchecked like a tumbleweed through a western town, very *The Road.* The sad motherfucker leaning up against the wall, smoking a cigarette, and staring at the cracked and crumbling concrete, very *Book of Eli.*

The street ends at Times Square, once a mega-hub of awesomeness where cowboys played guitar in their underwear and an unceasing cavalcade of electric, sex-themed ads assaulted wayward tourists. It was now just a scene from *The Postman.* There weren't enough people to provide upkeep for the cities. Those that stayed did so because they had become ghosts themselves, haunted by the losses of The Drop. They stuck around, though no more food was coming, except for that which they grew themselves. Though the children didn't play hopscotch on the streets and the stoplights had been turned off, the ghosts remained, remembering the glory of New York and its eight-and-a-half-million residents.

Glass crunches under my boots as I turn and look inside the Disney Store... all those toys just sitting there, no one left to play with them. I step inside. The cash register was busted open a long time ago, but the toys sit waiting. And I can't help but wonder who will actually benefit from the story that I am going to tell.

The next generation, I suppose, the ones that will grow up without music. The ones that will grow up without the internet, they'll want these dolls. They'll want something to play with.

I exit the Disney Store, sick of looking at clownish, Dory plush dolls. I am in time for the show. The man at the end of the street puts a gun in his mouth and pulls the trigger. Blood sprays the wall behind him. I scream like a maniac, but somehow, no one in Times Square hears me... because I'm the only person left alive in a place that was once called "The Crossroads of the World." And I wonder, was that man just waiting for someone to stumble along? Was he waiting for an audience before he killed himself? Or were his sixty days up?

I shudder and call the police. "Hello?... Yeah, there's been a suicide in Times Square... What do you mean three hours?"

I hang up. I go back inside the Disney store, and I grab myself a Dory plushy, and I hold onto it for dear life as the man's blood and brains run down the wall. This was probably the worst vacation idea I had ever had.

Available on amazon!

Be sure to check out

The Abbey

By Jacy Morris

Here is a sneak preview:

THE ABBEY

PROLOGUE

He would make him scream. So far they had all
screamed, their unused voices quaking and cracking with
pain that was made even worse by the fact that they were
breaking their vows to their Lord, their sole reason for
existence. Shattering their vows was their last act on earth,
and then they were gone. Now there was only one left. A
lone monk had taken flight into the abbey's lower regions, a
labyrinthine winding of corridors and catacombs lined with
the boxed up remains of the dead and their trinkets.

Brenley Denman's boots clanked off of the rough-
hewn, blue stone as he trounced through the abbey's crypts,
following the whiff of smoke from the monk's torch and the
echo of his harried footsteps. His men were spread out
through the underworks, funneling the monk ahead of
them, driving him the way hounds drove a fox. The monk
would lead them to his den, and then the prize would be
theirs. And then the world.

He held his torch up high, watching the flames
glimmer off of golden urns and silver swords, ancient relics
of a nobility that had long since gone extinct, their glory
only known by faded etchings in marble sarcophagi, the
remaining glint of their once-prized possessions, and the
spiders who built their webs in the darkness. Once they
were done with the monk, they would take anything that
glittered, but first they needed the talisman, the fabled
bauble that resided at the bottom of the mountain the abbey
was built on.

Throughout the land, legends of the talisman had been told for decades around hearthfires and inns throughout the isles. Then the tellers had begun to vanish, until the talisman of Inchorgrath and its stories had all but been forgotten. But Denman knew. He remembered the stories his father had told him while they sat around the fire of their stone house, built less than ten yards from the cemetery. His father's knuckles were cracked and dried from hours in the elements digging graves and rifling pockets when no one was looking. He knew secrets when he saw them. His father had first heard the story from the old Celts, the remains of the land's indigenous population, reduced to poverty and begging in the streets. His father said the old Celts' stories were two-thirds bullshit and one-third truth. They told of a relic, a key to the Celts' uprising and reclamation of the land, buried in the deepest part of the tallest mountain on the Isles. Of course, they spoke of regeneration and the return of Gods among men as well, but the relic... that was the important part. That was the part that was worth money. And now, he was here, with his men, ready to make his fortune.

He heard shouts, but it was impossible to tell where they were coming from. Sound echoed and bounced off of the blue, quartzite stone blocks, warping reality. He chose the corridor to his right, quickening his pace, his long legs eating up the distance. His men knew not to start without him, but you never knew when a monk would lash out, going against their discipline and training and earning a sword through the throat for their duplicity. That would be unacceptable to Denman. The monk must scream before he died.

His breathing quickened along with his pace, and he could feel the warmth of anticipation spread through his limbs as his breath puffed into the cold crypt air. Miles... they had come miles through these crypts, twisting and turning, burrowing into the secret heart of the earth, chasing the last monk who skittered through the hallways like a spider. The other monks had all known the secret of the abbey, the power it harbored, the relic it hid in its bowels. To a man, they had sat on their knees, their robes collecting condensation in the green grass of the morning, refusing to divulge the abbey's mysteries.

They had died, twisted, mangled and beaten. But still, all he could pull from them were the screams, musical expulsions of the throat that he ended with a smile as he dragged the razor-fine edge of his knife across their throats. Their blood had bubbled out, vivid against the morning sun, to splash on the grass.

When there was only one left, they had let him go. The youngest monk in the abbey, grown to manhood, but still soft about the face, his intelligent eyes filled with horror, stood and ran, his robe stained with the pooled blood of the monks that had died to his left and right. He was like one of the homing pigeons they used in the lowlands, leading them to home... to the relic. They had chased him, hooting and hollering the whole way, their voices and taunts driving the monk before them like a fox. The chase would end at his burrow; it always did.

Ahead, he heard laughing, and with that Denman knew that the chase was at an end. He rounded one last corner to see the monk being worked over by his men, savage pieces of stupidity who were good for two things, lifting heavy objects and killing people. Denman waved his hand and they let the suffering monk go. The monk sagged to the ground, his head bent over, his eyes leaking tears. He sobbed in silence.

Denman stood in the secret of the crypt, a room at the heart of the mountain, the place where legends hid. How deep had they gone? At first there had been stairs, but then they had reached a deeper part of the crypt where the corridors twisted and turned, the floor pitched ever downward. Time and distance had lost all meaning in the breast of the world. How long had it taken them to carve this place, the monks working in silence to protect their treasure? Hundreds of years? A thousand?

The room was simple and small, as the order's aesthetics demanded, filled by Denman and the nine men that he had brought to take the abbey's secrets. Wait, one was missing. He looked at his men, brutal pieces of humanity, covered in dirt, mud and blood. The boy wasn't there. Denman shrugged. He would find his way down eventually.

The walls of the room were blue-gray, stone blocks stacked one on top of the other without the benefit of mortar, the weight of the mountain providing the only glue that was needed. The only other features of the room were an alcove with two thick, tallow candles in cheap tin holders and an ancient oak table.

The smoke from his men's torches hung in the air, creating a stinging miasma that stung his eyes. Brenley Denman squatted next to the monk and used his weathered hand to raise the monk's head by his chin. He looked into the monk's eyes, and instead of the fear that he expected to see, there was something else.

"What is this? Defiance?" he asked, amused by the monk's bravado. Denman stood and kicked the monk in the mouth with his boot, a shit-covered piece of leather that was harder than his heart; teeth and blood decorated the stones.

"Where is it?" he asked the monk. There was no answer. Denman had expected none. Say what you will about the Lord's terrestrial servants, but they were loyal... which made everything more difficult... more exhilarating. Denman was a man that loved a challenge.

He handed his torch to one of his men, a broken-faced simpleton whose only gifts were strength and the ability to do what he was told. Denman knew that he would need both hands to make the monk sing his secrets.

"Hand me the Tearmaker," he said to another of his men. Radan, built like a rat with stubby arms and powerful legs, reached to his belt and produced a knife, skinny and flexible, designed not so much for murder as it was for removing savory meat from skin and fat. It made excellent work of fish, and it would most likely prove delightfully deft at making a tight-lipped monk break his vows.

As he reached out to take the proffered knife from his man, the monk scrambled to his feet and dove for the alcove. Before they could stop him, the monk grasped both of the candle sticks and yanked on them. The candlesticks rose into the air. Rusted, metal chains were affixed to their bases, and they clanked against the surrounding stone of the alcove as the monk pulled on them.

The distant sound of stones grinding upon stones reverberated throughout the crypt. Somewhere, something was moving. Denman glared at the monk. The robed figure dropped the candlesticks and turned to face them. With his head cast downward, he reached into the folds of his robe and produced a rosary. He folded his hands and began to pray, beads moving through his fingers, his lips moving without making sound.

The crypt shook as an unseen weight clattered through the halls of the crypt. Dust fell from the ceiling, hanging in the air, buoyed upwards by the tumbling smoke of their torches.

"What have you done?" Denman asked.

The monk did not respond. Instead, he reached into the hanging sleeve of one of his robes and produced a small stone thimble, roughly-made and ancient. It was shiny and black, the type of black that seemed to steal the light from the room. The monk put it up to his mouth, hesitated for a second and then swallowed it, grimacing in pain as the object slid down his throat.

In the hallway behind them, the grinding had stopped. The crypt was silent, but for the guttering of the torches and their own breathing. "Go see what happened," he said to the oaf and the rat. The other men followed them, leaving Denman alone with the monk and his unceasing, silent supplications to the Lord above.

Denman forced the monk onto the oak table. He offered little resistance. With Tearmaker in his hand, Denman began to carve the skin lovingly off of the monk's fingers. First, he carved a circle around the man's fingers, then a line. With the edge of his knife, he prodded a corner of the skin up, and then, grasping tightly, he ripped the skin away from the muscle and bone, dropping the wet flesh onto the ground. He did this to each finger, one by one. Sweat stood out on Denman's brow, and the monk had yet to scream. He hadn't so much as gasped or hissed in pain. He was turning out to be more work than he was worth. Except for the blood pulsing from his skinned fingers, he appeared to be asleep, his eyes softly closed.

"Where is it, you bastard?" There was no response but for the bleeding.

Denman pulled the monk's robe up around his waist. It was a quick jump, but he was eager to be done with the man on the table. Usually, he would take his time with a challenge like the monk, savoring the sensation of skin ripping from muscle and bone, but he could feel the weight of the mountain about him, its walls shrinking with every minute. Sweat covered his body, and the monk's calm demeanor was unnerving.

Radan rounded the corner at a run, his body dripping with sweat and panic on his face. He skidded to a stop, his boots grinding dust into the blue stones. "We're sealed in here," he said.

Denman looked at the monk lying on the table. His hand gripped Tearmaker tight. "What have you done?" The monk lay there, his eyes closed, a look of peace on his face. "What have you done!" he screamed, jabbing the knife into the monk's ribs. Then Denman saw the monk's hands.

Where before his index and pointer finger had been reduced to skinless chunks of muscle and bone dripping blood on the table, there was now skin. "Impossible," Denman whispered.

The monk's eyes snapped open, and finally, Denman got the scream that he had been waiting for.

Available on amazon!

Be sure to check out

THE PIED

PIPER

OF HAMELIN

By Jacy Morris

Here is a sneak preview:

The Pied Piper of Hamelin

Prologue: The River Weser

The boat captain sailed down the river, the wind ruffling his long, salt-and-pepper locks. It was a fine day. His ship was laden with goods, and he was relishing the prospect of turning a nice profit for himself and his crew. He should have been happy, ecstatic, singing shanties that would turn a barmaid's face red, but he wasn't.

The captain sniffed inward, pulling a grimy film of mucus into the back of his throat. He hacked up a thick glob and deposited it into the Weser River. He could taste the blood in it. His men were no better. Though they were ill, they still did their jobs. After all, a boatswain who couldn't earn his keep wouldn't receive his full share. On top of that, as an example to his men, the captain continued to work, stalking the decks and shouting out orders, though all he wanted to do was go down below and curl up in his cabin. He felt as if his head was trying to split in half, and he had an uncomfortable swelling in his groin that sent sharp pains through his entire body every time he moved.

Out of the corner of his eye, he spied furtive movement. Goddamn rats, he thought to himself. He would have to see if he could find some sort of boat cat in the next town. He consulted his charts, hand-drawn, passed down from captain to captain, and saw that the next village would be Hamelin.

It was an uppity berg; the mayor was trying to turn it into Rome from what the goodfolk at the pier told him. They had no need of Rome in this part of the world. What they needed was good strong ale, women with weak morals, and more good strong ale. Or maybe that's just what he needed.

A chilly breeze washed over the river, and the captain pulled his jacket tighter, gritting his teeth at the sharp pain the movement caused him. Underneath his arms, there were more swellings, unnatural lumps that seemed as if they were nothing but bundles of nerves. Pulling the jacket tighter had been like jabbing a flame-heated knife, point first, into each of his armpits.

Without warning, he began to cough like he had never coughed before. Black spots swam in front of his eyes, and for a brief moment, he thought, This is it. This is how I die. But then the coughing passed, and he was able to grab a raspy breath of air. The muscles in his back felt worse for wear, and he spat a wad of red-flecked phlegm into the river.

The breeze kicked up again, but this time, he didn't bother to readjust his jacket. Instead, he let the wind wash over him, evaporating the fever sweat from his brow.

"Captain," his first mate said, "Old Gert is dead."

It took a while for the words to sink into his fever-addled mind, but when they did, he did the only thing he could do. "Pitch him over the side, lad. It's a water-burial for him."

Normally, they would keep the body in the cold hull of the ship so that his family could bury him proper, but with all of the rats on board, it would be more dignified to give him to the river than to let those furry bastards make a meal out of him.

The first mate scuttled off to do his bidding without question. That was good. It meant that the crew didn't think he was responsible for the plague that had descended upon them. Sailors were a superstitious lot, but the captain had never held stock with the ridiculous notions of superstition. But that didn't mean that his crew wouldn't turn on him if more started to die.

He heard the sound of scurrying across the deck. "What the hell was that?" he wondered aloud. Spinning around quickly, he caught sight of movement out of the corner of his eye. It was another rat, a huge one. He chased it across the deck for a few steps, but then stopped due to the pain. After the first couple of steps, the lumps in his groin shot fire through his entire body. He vowed to find a cat when they got to Hamelin. In the meantime, he said a prayer for Old Gert as his body splashed into the river.

The rats watched and listened, the fleas on their backs oblivious to everything but the flesh in front of them and the blood underneath.

Available on amazon!

Printed in Great Britain
by Amazon